Praise for Chris D.'s novel NO EVIL STAR

"A healthy authorial sense of curiosity and generosity lends weight to No Evil Star's *intersecting lives, where Chris D. ably traces out the contours of human torment in a manner recalling American films of the 1970s."*

– Grace Krilanovich, author of
THE ORANGE EATS CREEPS

Praise for Chris D.'s DRAGON WHEEL SPLENDOR and Other Love Stories of Violence and Dread

"Every story delivers a gut punch...Chris D. writes with a clarity so merciless, reality itself seems to shimmer with menace... His sentences evoke the dark truths of a David Goodis and the savage humanity of a 21st century Dostoyevsky or Zola. Already a cult icon, with Dragon Wheel Splendor *the great Chris D. should finally find the audience he deserves. This is a book that can kill the voices in your head – or make you love them."*

– Jerry Stahl, author of
PLAINCLOTHES NAKED, PAINKILLERS
and PERMANENT MIDNIGHT

"Chris D. is someone who takes his dreams seriously, for, as Delmore Schwartz said, In Dreams Begin Responsibilities. To that end, Chris D.'s Los Angeles of the mind is awash with a heady mix of forlorn delirium, nostalgia pangs, seductive ghosts, and dangerous desires."

– Grace Krilanovich, author of
THE ORANGE EATS CREEPS

What Writers Had to Say About Chris D.'s Anthology
A MINUTE TO PRAY, A SECOND TO DIE

"Reading Chris D's blood-on-the-page prose is like running naked, screaming with terror and desire, through the fetid back alleys of American pulp culture. You're seduced, fucked over, doused with whiskey, set on fire, dragged by the getaway car, nailed by the hail from a 30.06 and still, still – you can't stop reading."

– Eddie Muller, author of
DARK CITY DAMES, THE ART OF NOIR and
the novels, THE DISTANCE and SHADOW BOXER

"...he continues a tradition in writing that is all but lost; authors who use their powers of imagination and creativity rather than simply recounting or inventing a memoir. Like the outsider artists that Chris D. champions, he writes for the future, for art, to someday be truly discovered for the great talent he is."

– John Doe, singer/songwriter
of X and The Knitters

"Chris D. presents...such an immense encapsulation of his life's work that it reads as literary autopsy of a man not yet dead but of one who has died a thousand times and somehow miraculously between crucifixions used pen as shovel to prevent himself from being buried alive."

– Lydia Lunch, musician and author of
PARADOXIA and WILL WORK FOR DRUGS

"To my mind, the lyrics he wrote...are as blinding a display of raw, universe-gobbling intelligence as have ever been penned...The sources from which Chris drew his inspiration are a classic pop cultural blend – exploitation films of all stripes, pulp fiction, French decadent poets, hot rod gangs, mystical Catholicism, underground biker comix, beatnik

booze into the hippie acid continuum, and on and on and on. This is a mix that has gained great subterranean currency over the past few decades, but when Chris was churning through these waters, they were as yet uncharted. His written work (along with that of fellow travelers such as Exene Cervenka, Dave Alvin, John Doe and Claude 'Kickboy' Bessy) created a new, totally crazed hipster aesthetic that rejected punk orthodoxy in favor of something much more magnificent and inclusive."

– Byron Coley, writer for WIRE Magazine,
author of C'EST LA GUERRE:
EARLY WRITINGS 1978-1983
and co-author (with Thurston Moore)
of NO WAVE: POST-PUNK.
UNDERGROUND. NEW YORK. 1976-1980.

NO EVIL STAR

Also by Chris D.

Double Snake Bourbon

A Minute to Pray, A Second to Die

Dragon Wheel Splendor and Other Love Stories of Violence and Dread

Mother's Worry

Shallow Water

Volcano Girls

Tightrope on Fire

Non-Fiction

Outlaw Masters of Japanese Film

Gun and Sword: An Encyclopedia of Japanese Gangster Films 1955-1980

NO EVIL STAR

a novel

by

Chris D.

A POISON FANG BOOK

If you enjoy this book, tell someone about it.

A POISON FANG BOOK

Front and back cover designs by C. D.

ISBN 978-0615868707

First published by New Texture, December 2011

Poison Fang Books edition published October, 2013

Printed in the United States

10 9 8 7 6 5 4 3 2 1

For Shepherd, Ben and Erika, who helped me through the rough summer of 2009

and

For Donna (again)

and

For VM, who inadvertently inspired this story

1

Blood-red bats. He hadn't seen them in months, and here they were back again, fluttering, swooping and swarming in the violet sky. He stared up through the tangled branches of the jungle outside Saigon and shaded his eyes. Somewhere in the basement of his mind, he knew it couldn't be Saigon. It had been nearly 15 years since he'd been there. But those damn little red sons-of-bitches did it every time. Confused him, made him think it was 1975 right before the pullout, not 1989 in dirty New York streets.

He shook his head violently, then stood stock-still. It didn't clear. The sky remained that soft, liquid lavender. The bats, though still a viscous-looking scarlet, had blurred, vibrating into indefinable little blobs gliding against the yellow clouds. Suddenly there was a loud screeching, a whoosh and everything in front of him burst into a grey static, like someone was tightening a thin electric metal band around the top of his skull. He blinked, and twin, ten-ton iron shutters slammed open-and-closed-and-open again on top of his cheekbones. Still, the vision wouldn't dissipate. He nearly mouthed a silent prayer, but caught himself and stopped short. Laughing soundlessly, he closed his eyes as he sat down on a raised hard ridge of packed earth that was like concrete beneath him. His head sank down between his shoulders. A dark warm pool of burnt sienna was all there was, lapping against the inside of his eyelids, lulling him into a false sense of security, of warmth and simulated oblivion.

"Goddamn it, Milo! I bet you haven't heard a single, solitary, goddamn word I've said."

The voice sounded familiar.

When he opened his eyes, the first thing he saw was the dead kitten lying in the gutter between his feet. It had been white at one time, but no longer. A rainbow-highlighted patina of black grease matted the fur. The closed right eye and the black blood-encrusted left socket, the scraped pink nose and the open mouth of the poor, pathetic creature broke him down. He hardened his heart as a twinge of hopelessness opened like a sucking chest wound right in the core of his being.

"Wake the fuck up! What-the-hell are you staring at?"

Milo straightened in his sitting position on the curb, gazing straight ahead across the swirl of traffic.

Edgy and irritated, Dave shuffled nearer, absent-mindedly scratching the day's growth of grey beard that covered his craggy face. He peered over Milo's shoulder and caught sight of the dead kitten.

"Aw, shit. What a shame." He clapped Milo on the back and leaned his face down close, then whispered in his ear, "Oh, well. The future looks bright, don't it?"

Milo shrugged Dave's clammy hand off his shoulder and stood up. He turned around. The pigeons were pigeons again. Flying rats, not bats. They fretted and strutted across the littered plaza outside St. Margaret's, totally oblivious to the herds of mid-afternoon pedestrians towering over them on the sidewalk. Milo raised his eyes, shielding them from the glare of the smoggy sun that was bisected by the steeple of the cathedral.

"That's life in the big shitty. It don't have to be that way, though."

Milo looked vacantly at Dave.

Dave considered himself a hardass, as did many other people who had the dubious fortune to know him. But he wilted and became sheepish under what he imagined to be Milo's piercing stare. Nervously, he smoothed his greying, greasy mane, and then tucked both his hands in the pockets of his Army camouflage jacket.

Milo lit a cigarette, inhaled deeply, slowly let out the smoke.

Dave decided to reopen his attack, but couldn't quite look Milo in the eye. Instead, he stared down at his friend's partially unbuttoned shirt.

"Have you given my proposition any more thought?"

Milo took another quick drag, threw the half-smoked butt on the walk and ground it under his heel. "What proposition is that?" he innocently teased.

"You know goddamn well what I'm talking about. You've been down there." Suddenly, Dave realized he was shouting. He paused for a second, darting a gaze behind him, then swiveled his head round, stepping only a few inches from Milo's face. His voice lost volume but none of its intensity. "You've been down there in the cellar…" He wagged his head towards the church. "You know, down in the fucking catacombs."

"C'mon, Dave. Don't exaggerate. There aren't any catacombs in St. Margaret's."

Dave grimaced. "All right. You know what I mean. The basement. You know what's down there. You know I'm not just blowing smoke up your ass."

Milo shook his head and turned away.

"Okay, okay. Fine. Shine me on. Go ahead. Ungrateful bastard."

The last words stung, and Milo reluctantly looked into Dave's angry eyes.

"You shouldn't take it that way, Dave." Milo frowned, then suddenly remembered and glanced at his watch. "Look, man, I got to go. I told the Monsignor I'd only be out here for a few minutes to have a smoke."

"Whatever. Go back in. I swear to God! Is that what we were fighting for over in Nam? Because if it was, I should have just let Jerry blow both our goddamn heads off."

"You don't know what you're talking about."

"Oh, yeah? I don't know what I'm talking about? At least I'm not sleeping in a cubbyhole in the wall that smells like incense and holy water 24-7! Man, that coma, that fucking speedball did you worse than your whole tour in Nam. You're right out of some goddamn storybook. That Monsignor is your goddamn Curé and you're his Quasimodo."

Milo sighed. "I'll talk to you later, Dave."

Milo's room – if you could even call it a room it was so small – was dark and damp, lit only by a yard-wide, foot-tall, deeply-recessed window. The opening was at Milo's eye level, but the chamber made up part of the cathedral's cellar so on the exterior façade it was only a few inches above the ground and partially obscured by withered rosebushes.

Milo took a deep breath, plucked a cigarette from his mouth, flicked it outside and turned away. He surveyed the narrow chamber, then sank down on the metal cot that was squeezed up against the sweating, grey stone wall. Leaning over to his left, he spat into the ancient sink that jutted out a couple of feet from the opposite wall and was mere inches from his face. He turned the loose-fitting handle on the lone cold-water spigot, scooped some of the liquid onto his face, shut it off, then let his head plop down on the pillow.

Dave's petulant outburst rang in his head. "At least I'm not sleeping in a cubbyhole in the wall that smells like incense and holy water 24-7! Man, that coma, that fucking speedball did you worse than your whole tour in Nam."

There was a deafening blare of a truck horn, the smell of burning diesel and the chatter of an old Vietnamese woman. And he was in Saigon again.

He found himself standing on a busy, reeking thoroughfare. It was a beautiful day, at least as far as he was concerned in his self-contained world. Sunny, not too warm, a gentle breeze and no Cong blowing themselves up for that last week.

Then something had caught his attention across the street – it looked like Dave sitting at a front table on the sidewalk, reading a French newspaper in the open-air patio of the restaurant on the corner. Dave had been much more clean-cut then. He had looked a lot like what he was – a black-bag man for Army Intelligence. He didn't try to hide his calling. In fact, he had delighted in flaunting it, something his superiors frowned upon but tolerated because he was so damn good at what he did, so relentlessly ruthless, cold-blooded and sociopathic. Swiveling his head almost imperceptibly, Dave had glanced at Milo, then casually returned his attention to the newspaper as if he hadn't seen him.

Milo smiled to himself. Clutching the carton of cigarettes and the tiny box, he crossed through the slow-moving traffic and dove into the steep, shadowy staircase between Lucky's bar and the restaurant. No MPs around, just the way he liked it. He ran all the way up to the top, paused before the glass fire extinguisher case and then stopped, catching his breath and admiring his reflection.

He had rigorously kept up his appearance back then. His corporal's uniform was spotless and well pressed, his ash blonde hair oiled and combed straight back, his face smoothly shaven, even in the shallow cleft of his chin. He had smirked, given himself a mock salute, then looked embarrassed as he suddenly spotted the decrepit old woman staring as she ambled towards him in the gloomy, fetid smelling hallway.

Smiling sheepishly, he nodded to her as he passed, then automatically lurched to a halt and rapped lightly on Lucky's door. He thought he heard her footsteps, the slap of her bare feet on the wood and linoleum floor but couldn't be sure because right then a cacophony of voices welled up from somewhere in the bowels of the building.

Abruptly, the door was thrown open by a petite, frail Vietnamese woman with bleached-blonde hair. She leaned one hand against the doorjamb and jauntily propped the other on one of her narrow hips.

"Aren't you gonna invite me in?"

Lucky finally gave him the faintest hint of a smile, then folded her arms as she turned sideways to let him pass. Once he cleared the entrance, she languidly pressed the door closed.

He was a lot later than he had said he would be.

"What's shakin', honey?"

"Your dick?" she answered with sarcastic vigor.

He rolled his eyes, shook his head good-naturedly, ready to bear the brunt of her considerable temper. "Okay, okay. What's up, baby?"

"Milo, what's my name?"

"What're you talking about?"

"My name. What is it?"

"Lucky…" He paused, feeling the same embarrassment he had felt on the landing, but he shrugged it off. "Hey, come here. You know you're my girl."

She grimaced, shuffling over to him. Once she came into reach, they spontaneously grabbed each other, embracing, kissing open-mouthed. For a few seconds it seemed they would end up right there on the floor, fucking each other's brains out. But, almost simultaneously, that diseased other part of their souls kicked in.

They came up for air. "I love you, baby."

She started to push him away. "Yeah, right."

"Stop that. You know I want to bring you back to the States with me."

"And what do we do about Jerry? He's not going to be happy. He'll never let me go. He can make a lot of trouble for you, for both of us. He likes being an MP."

"Fuck him!"

She eyed him cynically.

"Don't worry, honey. I'll take care of him when the time

comes. We play it right, we'll be gone before he even knows it. We'll get hitched before we split from here. Then you won't have any trouble getting in. Before you know it, we're back in the Big Apple."

"Yeah…then I can turn tricks in – what you call it…Alphabet City? While you cop dope, right?"

"I told you, it's not gonna be that way. We'll both get clean when we get back. You know, it's just over here you gotta stay high. Stay high or you go nuts."

"Or maybe you go nuts because you are high all the time. Did you ever think of that? Don't make stupid excuses for what we're doing!"

He rolled his eyes at her reproach, slammed his back against the wall of the narrow entranceway and looked up at the ceiling. "Fuck!"

She sighed, took a deep wheezing breath and leaned her head against his chest. "Did you bring it?"

He lifted her sweet face by her delicate chin and kissed her quickly.

She took the carton of cigarettes from him and, not even looking, tossed it carelessly behind her onto the mattress on the floor. Her petulant impatience had made him smile. But then, as he had opened the almost microscopic box, which held several little glassine envelopes of heroin, something happened which was emblazoned in his memory. He wasn't sure why, but it still haunted him. The look on her face. A bizarre mingling of ecstasy and disgust had spread across her features, an unholy shadow of naked, ugly need that had simultaneously scared him and made his dick hard. The thought shamed him even now. It was that direct conduit to darkness that made the empty hole open up again inside of him and start to suck at his core.

She had shifted her dark violet eyes to peer into his, smiling faintly, as if dazed. Then suddenly the smile had disappeared into a neutral expression that shocked him with its vacancy and despair. Turning her back on him, she had walked straight over to the open window that looked out over the noisy street.

He only paused for a few seconds staring after her, then plopped down on their makeshift excuse for a bed, carefully withdrawing an envelope. He was pretty fanatical about cleanliness – at least compared to the garden-variety junkie – and reached into his pants pocket, pulling out a handful of sealed syringes he had stolen from the medic supply in his outfit. He was so used to it all by then, his hands moved as if they had a mind of their own. He prepared their fixes quickly in the blackened spoon, opened a fresh bottle of water and cooked up the whole mess with his Zippo. He hadn't noticed her sit down beside him, but when he felt her frail, translucent hand perch softly on his shoulder, he was not surprised. He slowly turned his face to look into her eyes, mere inches from his. He was disturbed to see them welling up, but he bit his tongue and said nothing.

"Do me first," she whispered.

He handed her the syringe and watched, devoid of feeling, as she pulled up the cutoff denim shorts on one leg and found her usual vein. It opened like a hungry mouth, spewing almost black blood into the plastic cylinder as it registered. Slowly, tenderly, she drove the plunger home, swiftly withdrew it with an involuntary gasp, then thrust it out for him to take from her. He picked it from between her nicotine-stained fingers and watched absent-mindedly as she swatted the little drop of blood that had remained on the surface of her inner thigh.

"You should be careful, honey, shooting there. Keep yourself nice and clean. You don't want to get an abscess and go septic."

She had smiled at his concern. But he had already looked away from her, getting his own shot set to go.

The smack hit them hard. It was twice as strong as anything in the States. Not that he would have known that, since he'd only done it for the first time there in Nam. For an indeterminate while they lolled in each other's arms on the lumpy mattress. At the time, it seemed like hours. But he had realized later it must have been only a few minutes. After the glow of the initial rush faded, they fell on each other like hungry animals, ripping off each other's clothes and quickly coupling. They couldn't come because of the dope, but having an orgasm didn't matter to either of them. She could get him hard like no one else, except for maybe his high school sweetheart, Anne. He shared an immense pleasure with Lucky in just being able to fuck like that for seemingly hours on end.

What he hadn't known at the time was that something was happening downstairs.

Dave was still installed at his table in the open-air café. No longer reading his paper, he was just sitting, staring off into nowhere while he nursed his Pernod and an evil-smelling Japanese cigarette. Something registered on the periphery of his vision. He shifted his gaze almost imperceptibly to watch the American Army jeep pull up to the curb right in front of the entrance to Lucky's building. It was her ersatz boyfriend Jerry, the MP, in full regalia. Even from where Dave was sitting, he could see Jerry had an awfully strange look on his face. The blood had drained out of his hands, neck and forehead, but his cheeks, nose and ears were flushed fire-engine red. Dave had had the funny impression steam was shooting out of Jerry's ears. But the amusement abruptly faded as he watched Jerry just sit there in an indecisive stupor.

Upstairs, Milo was slumped across the mattress with his back against the wall. He had just pulled on his pants and was watching naked Lucky perched cross-legged on the edge of the mattress with another spoonful of smack cradled in her lap. She carefully pressed the needle of the syringe into the cotton and sucked the fix up into the rig.

"Don't slam too much, honey. It's stronger than you think."

"Shut up..." she smiled without looking at him, "…my dearest darling."

Suddenly, there was a loud crunch, then a bang as the apartment door was slammed off its hinges, crashing to the floor. Milo pushed away from the wall, reaching out for Lucky's shoulder. By the time they raised their heads to look, Jerry was standing in front of them with his .45, drawn and cocked.

"Oh, man! Oh, God! Oh, man!"

"Jerry –" Milo slowly raised up one hand.

"Fuck-a-duck!"

"Jerry, hold on a second – "

"This is really rich!" Jerry shook his head, as if trying to clear it. "I knew…I knew it was you she was seeing, Milo."

Lucky whispered softly, "Jerry, put that gun down…"

"I'll put it down *on you,* bitch! Thought I didn't know, hunh? I knew you were getting strung out, honey!" He kicked at the spoon that Lucky had set on the grimy, green linoleum floor, and it clattered into the corner. "Look at *that!* Caught red-handed!"

Lucky reached up toward the gun barrel. "Jerry, listen…"

"Don't move another inch, honey…"

She froze. Milo's eyes darted around the room. He had foolishly not brought his gun with him. What could he use for a weapon? He glanced sideways at Lucky. The pendant around her neck caught the light and reflected into Jerry's eyes.

"What's that?"

"What's what, honey?"

"Don't 'honey' me, you goddamn, yellow bitch! You know goddamn well what! That evil piece of shiny shit hanging around your scrawny neck! Who gave you that?"

"I told you –"

Abruptly, Jerry yanked it off with his left hand, studying it while keeping an eye on the both of them.

"I told you, Jerry, last week. The last time you asked me. My brother gave it to me. It's a good-luck charm."

Milo watched a thread-thin line of blood well up on the back of her neck where the pendant chain had broken the skin.

"Please, give it back. It means a lot to me." Slowly, she raised her hand out to him again.

"I told you not to move," he sobbed. Without warning, the muzzle exploded. Milo caught Lucky as she was thrown backwards. A large, jagged hole blossomed in the center of her emaciated chest. She made an involuntary gasp, sucking in air, and a dark red audibly gurgled from the wound. She violently pitched her head forward, vomiting up a handful of blood.

Milo had known she was going quickly. His most vivid memory now was of having wanted to whisper the words, "I love you," in her ear. She had been only an inch away from his lips. But he had choked as he tried to get the words out, had gagged and almost threw up himself.

He grasped the back of her skull to hold her head, but he could see from the glassy look in her eyes that she was already gone. Gently, he lay her down on the mattress. Then, with a deliberate slowness, he turned his ashen face up to look at her killer.

Jerry was dumbstruck. Staring down at Lucky's corpse, he wasn't ready for Milo springing, tackling him, smashing him into the opposite wall.

Milo didn't remember much about what happened in the next few seconds, because his anger was so overwhelming. It had felt as if someone had rammed a hot poker into his brain, and he was literally seeing red as he choked Jerry's purple, swollen neck. Somehow Jerry raised his gun arm, even though Milo had it pinned against the crumbling plaster with his elbow, and there was a popping sound muffled by his own flesh. A searing flame shot through his left shoulder right down through his elbow to the tips of his fingers, and Jerry catapulted them both away, tumbling, spinning. They landed, with Milo sandwiched between, Jerry on top and Lucky's body beneath him on the bloody mattress. Jerry made a horrible, nightmare noise – half-screaming, half-growling – as he pressed the gun barrel against Milo's temple.

There was another deafening report and, at first, Milo thought that Jerry had fired. But Jerry abruptly went limp, collapsing his full weight on Milo's chest.

Milo heaved him off, then spotted Dave standing over them, slowly lowering his own smoking automatic.

"You gotta get the fuck out of here, my friend. Pronto." Dave tucked the gun nonchalantly into his belt. He reached out a hand to pull Milo up.

Once Milo was vertical, he had felt incredibly faint, probably as much from the violent struggle and the heroin as having been shot point blank in the shoulder. Dave steadied him as he grabbed Lucky's long silk scarf from the back of the straight back chair and tied it tightly around Milo's wound, skillfully fashioning a tourniquet bandage. He fished a card and a pen out of his shirt pocket and quickly scrawled a phone number and address on the back. "Get over there and lie low. Keep your mouth shut. I'll be over in a while after I clear this up."

As if on cue, sirens welled up a couple of blocks away. Dave gestured towards the open window. Milo followed his movement, stared dumbly out over the stinking, steaming back alley and the bunched-together tenement rooftops.

"You've gone this route plenty of times before when Jerry was coming up the stairs. Nothing new. Unfortunately, today you're just making it a little later than usual."

Milo stared at Lucky and Jerry. If it hadn't been for the gaping maw of coagulating blackness in Lucky's chest, the bloody hole drilled in Jerry's helmet, the two could have been a couple taking an afternoon nap.

Milo crouched down, painfully grabbed his shirt from under Lucky's legs, hoisted it up and slipped it on. Pressing his foot down on Jerry's left wrist, he pried open the dead, already stiffening fist, then delicately looped Lucky's pendant and chain around his fingers. Straightening up, his gorge rose, but he kept it down. His throat was parched, constricted, and hot tears welled up uncontrollably in his eyes.

"C'mon, man. Grieve later."

Milo threw one leg over the windowsill, looked down into the alley, then over at his friend.

"Thanks, Dave."

"Go!"

Blood on his palm made Milo slip as he went out the window, and he plummeted sideways down onto a tarpaulin covering three trash cans. The pain that ricocheted through his limbs and torso blinded him with a white-hot sheet of light that caused him to black out. When he came to a half a minute later, he saw Dave's face poking out of the window from the flight above, petulantly staring at him. Suddenly Dave's arm appeared and a stream of warm water splashed down from an upended drinking glass, dousing Milo's face. Dave vanished. Milo sat up, shook his head, then sprang to his feet.

An ancient, bald-pated man, a cigarette dangling from his non-existent lips, crouched against the opposite wall and indifferently watched him from beneath hooded lids. Ten yards beyond the man, Milo saw a jeep screech to a halt at the north end of the alley. A crowd was gathering out front. Milo casually turned on his heel and sauntered in the opposite direction.

Back in the cloistered cell in the bowels of St. Margaret, Milo let out a shuddering sigh. He tried to banish the vividness of Lucky's bloody corpse from his mind and turned on his side. But there it was, only a scant few feet from his eyes – a reminder. Lucky's pendant was hanging from the upper left corner of the cracked mirror above the rust-stained sink. Cast adrift, staring off into space, he reached up, grabbed it, then mindlessly slipped the chain around his neck and tucked the pendant beneath his shirt collar.

He gazed at the sweating, grey stone ceiling; then, before he knew it, briefly dropped off to sleep and dreamt that he was out of the little cloister in the cellars of St. Margaret, staying in a large, three-room loft in Soho. But it wasn't some gentrified artist's pad. There were ten other people living with him whom he hardly knew. They all shuffled about in ratty clothes and disintegrating shoes, and the place smelled of bacon and boiled cabbage. His gorge rose, and he woke with a start, bathed in a cold sweat. The prickly perspiration made him feel one with the stone walls. A piece of rock with no emotions. A cipher, a nothing man.

Living a paycheck away from being homeless, let alone abject poverty, didn't bother him, even living in that tiny room. What scared him was the prospect of having to one day live in a cramped apartment with other people he didn't know and didn't like. It was one of his few recurring nightmares not filled with Nam imagery. A recurring theme of being powerless over where he lived – but the places in the dreams were always different and so were the people in them.

An old-fashioned light bulb near the top of the wall next to the door started to flash, and a low buzzer sounded. Shit! Monsignor Aloysius was calling him.

2

The office of Monsignor Aloysius was tucked away on the ground floor in back of the sacristy, just before you left the church to make a short jaunt across an anemic strip of scrawny grass stubble to the rectory. Milo was always impressed by the sanctimonious duplicity employed by the architect, engineering the office entrance so the door appeared no more than an ornately carved wood panel in the wall, unless one's eyes were sharp and caught the glint of the tarnished brass doorknob in the shadows of the recessed alcove. Milo inhaled and exhaled deeply, looked up at the ceiling twenty feet above, shook his head to clear it and knocked.

"Come in, Milo."

Presumptuous bastard. He opened the door and winced at the intense prism of colors that hit him full in the face, the amplified late afternoon sunlight streaming through the stained glass window positioned just over the heads of the chamber's occupants.

The Monsignor was skulking behind his massive mahogany desk, holding forth and pontificating to three of the church's more upscale, late-middle-aged female parishioners. Milo knew the attractive Mrs. Reynolds. The other two he had not seen before, though he remembered their names from the Monsignor's afternoon agenda. Mrs. Ambrusco and Mrs. Carlton didn't look like they belonged in the same room with this more seductive creature. All three were in the neighborhood of 60 years old, but the gracefully voluptuous Mrs.

Reynolds looked ten years younger.

Monsignor Aloysius swiveled his grey head, his beady eyes squinting disapprovingly at Milo, and he abruptly sank into his chair. His long tapered hands nervously flexed and, finding each other in the middle of the cluttered desktop, clasped themselves into a tight fold of wrinkled parchment skin.

"I'm really rather disappointed, Milo."

Milo let the condescending tone slide past him.

"These fountain pens you brought me yesterday – I specifically asked you to try them out before you left them on my desk."

Milo glanced at the women, than back at his boss. "I did. They were all working."

Both Mrs. Ambrusco and Mrs. Carlton gave him smarmy, incredulous looks.

"These three fine ladies are amongst our most illustrious and generous parishioners."

Milo, in spite of himself, felt a mischievous, hand-caught-in-the-cookie-jar expression fighting to take possession of his face. He tried not to look at Mrs. Reynolds, who was smiling and studying him closely.

"They tithe regularly in rather large increments."

"Yes, sir," Milo obsequiously acknowledged.

"How am I to explain to them when I'm caught in the embarrassing position of giving them a token of our parish's grateful esteem, fountain pens, really what amount to no more than mere souvenirs of St. Margaret's Cathedral – though admittedly gold-plated," the priest grinned at the three women, before turning a melodramatic frown on Milo, " – and they won't even write."

"Monsignor?" It was Mrs. Reynolds. The priest obediently twisted round to her, and she switched on full throttle the arsenal of her formidable British charm. "I'm sure it was all a rather unfortunate mistake. It's very possible that the pens dried up overnight. It has been known to happen." With a small elegant movement, she tilted her head to face Milo and smiled seductively. "The weather *has* been *extremely* hot. And the humidity in the air is virtually *non-existent*."

It was all that Milo could do to fight off the slight smile forming at the corners of his lips. Her voice was liquid honey.

"Please don't be too hard on him. I know how hard he works here."

Following her lead, the Monsignor stared at Milo. He

grimaced, sighed and reluctantly gave ground, deferring to the charisma of this enchanting woman.

"Yes, I suppose anything is possible." His tone was sarcastic and resigned. "Milo, would you please be good enough to go downstairs and bring up three working fountain pens?"

Mrs. Reynolds smiled at Milo. He suppressed a grin as he silently opened the door and disappeared into the darkened vestibule.

The service closet in the basement was located several yards beyond his own room. It was on the same side of the narrow sepulcher-like passageway, cut and recessed into the ashen stone wall and sealed off by two massive oak doors that were padlocked at the bottom where they joined. Milo squatted, slipped his key in the rusty mechanism near the base, popped it open and out of its clasp, then tugged at the right door without standing up. He knelt as it swung to, and reached into the nearest box on the ground under the bottom shelf. He tested each pen on the cardboard side as he brought them out. Not surprisingly, he went through two more dried-up ones before he got the required trio. Just as he was shutting the closet and locking up, a familiar voice echoed faintly from down the corridor.

Milo straightened and moved silently through the shadows to the half-open door about five yards further into the void on the other side. He peered through the crack where the hinges meshed and saw Nunzio, the neighborhood mafia boss, clad in a smoking jacket, black corduroy trousers and his stocking feet. The bulky 65-year-old man was only 5'8" but projected a formidably vital presence. A phone receiver was in his right hand pressed against his ear while he compulsively rolled a smoldering cigar between the thumb and fingers of his left hand.

"That's right, honey. I call it my treasure chamber." His oily voice had a heavy Brooklyn accent, rasping from his throat in a seductive purr. "...you should come on down here sometime and see it all. Very valuable antiques, very valuable paintings. Really, you wouldn't believe it. Stuff I picked up during the war -- "

He paused, listening.

"No, World War Two. Not the fucking Vietnam War."

Nunzio paused again, listening, then abruptly looked toward the door.

"Hold on a sec, honey…" He put his hand over the receiver as he laid it down onto the blood-colored leather of the nearby easy chair. He crept quietly to the entrance and poked his head out, squinting into the shadows. There was no one. He ambled back leisurely, sliding his feet into worn moccasins on the Oriental rug as he picked up the phone.

"I'm back…no, no, it was nothing."

Milo stood in the shade against the grimy wall of the inner courtyard. He studied the red-coal tip of his half-gone cigarette as he inhaled.

He felt a prickly hurt deep between his ears, winced at the deafening whoop-whoop of the chopper blades, and the orange beacon on the bird's tail burst into a brilliant white concussion of olive shrapnel. It had happened so fast, it was a soundless abstract painted onto his retinas. An acrid blackness gradually greyed into a tropical twilight. A pit that hadn't been there before slowly materialized out of the smoke swirling around his feet. Don Bowman, the corporal who'd been a promising young architect before he was drafted, was a shredded doll at the bottom, pierced through with iron spikes.

"Milo…Milo?"

There was a delicious silky-throated sweetness in the words. He knew that voice -- a deep, smoky female tone with a slightly British accent.

"Earth to Milo…"

Abruptly he realized those weren't spikes piercing his partner's body, they were fountain pens…gold-plated fountain pens.

He blinked slowly and purposefully, and when his eyes came open again Mrs. Reynolds in her modestly low-cut summer dress was poised before him. Her fine skin glowed in the shadows. She was nearly in silhouette against the late afternoon sun that spilled in from the street. He could just make out her beguiling features. She smiled as she saw he was once again amongst the living, and he grinned back at her.

"Have an extra cigarette, friend?"

Milo nodded. As he pulled the pack from his top pocket, he noticed that Mrs. Ambrusco and Mrs. Carlton had just reached the plaza beyond. They were swiveling their heads to survey the busy avenue, searching for the chauffeured ride they'd shared. Mrs. Carlton turned in their direction and, seeing Mrs. Reynolds with Milo, she tapped her overweight comrade on the shoulder and gestured toward them.

"Don't look now, but your friends are getting an eyeful."

Mrs. Reynolds plucked a smoke from the pack, glanced over her shoulder as she lit it and laughed. She took a deep drag, then blew the smoke above Milo's head.

"Those sanctimonious hausfraus. They're not my friends. Let

them look."

"You're not worried about what they think?"

"You should know me better than that by now."

He propped one foot behind him against the wall and leaned back onto the cold stone. A gleeful smirk slowly took hold of her mouth, betraying her mischievous disdain for social niceties. She was a handful. But that was why he liked her. Though married, her elderly husband was out of town a lot, and she pretty much did what she wanted. In a discreet fashion. A vivid image of the first time he'd been to bed with her reared up before his eyes. He'd been doing her a favor – or rather the Monsignor a favor – fixing a loose railing on Mrs. Reynolds' penthouse balcony because her upscale building's maintenance man had suddenly taken sick. It had been a hot summer day the year before, much like that very afternoon. After he'd finished, he'd been wiping the rivulets of sweat running into his eyes from his forehead, loping wearily back into her bedroom still bare-chested. She'd been sitting on the edge of the huge bed in the shady coolness of the all-white chamber. When he'd let his hands drop from his face, he'd found himself staring into her eyes. There was an unmistakable lust in them. All she'd had on was his white-long sleeve shirt that he had left folded on the nearby chair. Very slowly, without breaking eye contact, she had flexed her left knee and raised her foot to perch on the mattress, revealing the smooth-shaven cleft between her legs. He'd walked right up to her and had not resisted as she undid his belt, unzipped his jeans and pulled him out into her hungry, waiting mouth. After a minute or two, he'd lifted her up and placed her on the floor at his feet. He'd pounded away at her on the deep fur rug for a good half hour.

The two women across the plaza had lost interest, distracted by their car pulling to the curb directly in front of them.

"I haven't seen too much of you."

She grimaced. "I know, darling. Harold's trip last week got called off, and he's not leaving again for another month."

He smiled.

She leered, full of coy mischief. "You're not cross with me, I hope?"

"Of course not."

She took another deep drag, then dropped it, nervously crushing the butt beneath one graceful foot. "Dear Monsignor Al probably wouldn't appreciate me doing that. Littering his precious yard."

"I sweep the walk three times a week."

She blushed. "Damn it, Milo, why do you stay here? You're so much better than this."

"It suits me."

"How can it? And how can you let him talk to you the way he does? It was all I could do to keep from exploding in there. He's just like those two bitches. A self-righteous hypocrite."

"Why do you keep coming back, if you can't stand him?"

She made a face and looked over at the church doors. "You know one of the small concessions I make to Harold is coming to Mass with him every Sunday. He doesn't ask much of me anymore, and I feel I owe it to his tolerant nature to humor him."

"Mrs. Reynolds –"

"Don't call me that. It makes me feel old. I've told you to call me Dorrie."

He lowered his voice. "I can't call you that when I'm around the church. It wouldn't be good for either one of us if somebody heard. We shouldn't even be talking here. Aloysius may step out any minute."

"Don't worry. His childhood mafia friend came in after you left, and the two of them went down to the basement."

Milo shifted his gaze to look at the rundown cathedral.

She studied his profile and restrained herself from reaching out to run her fingers along his unshaven face. "Why do you stay here?"

"Let's just say…I enjoy the Spartan life. It's a carry-over from the military. Besides, I owe the Monsignor."

"You owe him?"

"Something he did for my dad, right before he died during World War Two. And something else he did a few years ago. Something he did for me. I'll tell you about it sometime."

She gave him a thoughtful, indulgent smile. She started to raise her hand to stroke his cheek, then remembered where she was. She timidly glanced around, opened her purse and withdrew a lacy handkerchief in one quick motion, dabbing at her forehead, then her lips.

He watched her with affection.

"You must have been very young when your father died."

"I never got to meet him. I was born six months before my mother got the telegram." He looked down at his feet and watched a beetle slowly crawling along the edge of one cowboy boot. He carefully nudged it away toward the wall, concerned for its safety. She peered down to see what he was doing and felt a sudden pang of emotion at his sweetness. He noticed she was watching him and raised his head. “Fuck, he was pretty young himself. He was only 19. He’d only been in the Army a year.”

There was an uncomfortable few seconds of quiet between them.

“Well, Milo.” She gave him an exaggerated frown, trying to laugh and make light because she felt just the opposite. “I guess it’s time for me to be going.” She couldn’t sustain the act and suddenly her expression changed back. “I do miss you, you know.”

He nodded.

“I’ll get word to you soon.” She turned decisively, making herself march off. Just before she got to the edge of the plaza, she threw him a wry glance over her shoulder and gave him a wave.

Milo was tired, though he hadn’t done much of anything. Maybe he was depressed. Though the way he lived minute-to-minute now, it was kind of hard to tell.

3

Monsignor Aloysius and Nunzio stood in the cellar corridor, the priest wringing his hands and exuding considerably less self-confidence than earlier. His lined face was frozen with anxiety as he stared into space. Nunzio lit a fresh cigar and thoughtfully looked at his nervous friend. He inhaled deeply, then blew out a cloud of blue smoke.

"What? What is it? Are you finally going to tell me what's bothering you?"

Aloysius turned away, gulped, sweat beading his forehead.

Nunzio hung his head and shook it in disgust.

"What? You can't even talk to me anymore? We known each other since we were this high – " Nunzio gestured with the flat of his hand at the level of his waistline. "All the way through high school, then in a goddamn foxhole in Normandy."

He was losing his patience.

"Why are you sweating like that? I know it's summer, but it's like an icebox down here!" He surveyed the echoey cavern. "That's another reason I like comin' down to the basement. Nice and cool in summer."

The priest gave him a blank stare.

Nunzio rubbed his fingers on the bridge of his nose, trying to settle his erupting temper. He took a breath and sighed.

"C'mon, Al. What-the-hell? Is it that deadbeat Nam vet you keep on here? Out of the goodness of your heart?"

The Monsignor moved his lips, trying to talk. He shook his head, wheezed out several shallow breaths, then stammered, "His name's Milo. That's Harry's kid, Dom."

"Harry? What-the-fuck you talking about, Al? Harry's been dead nearly 45 years. Who cares if he's Harry's kid? He's middle-aged, cracked and can barely support himself."

Aloysius finally regained his composure. "I do, I care. Milo's the closest thing I'll ever have to a son. And after how Harry died…"

"Christ, you are a broken record!"

"You know – you know what I'm talking about. If we'd been paying attention instead of grabbing everything we could lay our hands on…" His querulous voice trailed off.

Nunzio jabbed one finger into Aloysius' chest. "Don't forget, Al, old Harry was doing some grabbing, too. If he hadn't been with us when the goddamn kraut sergeant burst in, he wouldn't've got it. He took his chances, just like you and me." He felt he was on a roller-coaster. He saw Al's pasty look and made a superhuman effort to quash his annoyance. When he spoke again, his voice had assumed a quality of tolerant gentleness at odds with his personality. "Look, Al. You know we're friends. I understand. I really do. But there's just so much I can take."

"I'm getting nervous about -- "

He exploded again. "About what! What-the-hell are you talking about?"

The priest abruptly got angry himself, something that startled Nunzio.

"Having all that stuff down here!"

Realizing where he was, he finished his sentence in whispered but still livid tones, "*All the stuff we took in the war*."

"You're puttin' me on, right? We've had it stashed down here for years, and just now you're startin' to get nervous?"

The troubled cleric shrank into himself. He knew he was no match for his domineering friend. Overcome with the futility of his guilt, of ever expiating it, he choked up and put one hand over his eyes. Realizing he'd gone too far, Nunzio draped a consoling arm around his old pal's shoulder.

"C'mon now, Al. Everything's okay. Go upstairs and lie down. You're done for the day, right?"

The Monsignor nodded. Dejectedly, he walked away into the shadows, not even looking back at his friend. Nunzio stood gazing after him. He made a clucking noise with his tongue as he dug in his pocket and brought out a rusty key. He shuffled to the heavy wooden door of his private chamber, unlocked it and entered the shadowy room. He ignited a wooden match by touching it to the one lone, lit candle, then glided over the deep pile rug to an elaborate, golden candelabra sitting on the table. Little by little, the room became illuminated with a warm glow as he swept the flame to each successive wick. Like a veil being lifted, the luster of the objects on the L-shaped mahogany slab fed off the candlelight: gold ingots, silver and gold plates, dishes, bowls, utensils, cups, all sitting on a black velvet tablecloth that gradually gave way to an ermine-lined bed of carefully laid-out jewelry – rings, bracelets and necklaces studded with diamonds, rubies, emeralds and sapphires. Behind it all, hanging from every inch of wall space, and just visible in the flickering dance of orange shadows, were paintings. They were masterworks long thought lost in Europe, art given over to and incinerated on the sacrificial funeral pyre of culture that was the Second World War.

Nunzio surveyed this ostentatious display with the kind of warmth one usually reserves for human affection. It was like a story-book. That's what it was – like a goddamn fairy tale. He still couldn't quite believe it. Sighing with pleasure, he stepped backward, aware of every inch of the floor behind him as he navigated in reverse and down into the depths of his plush, oxblood-colored easy chair. Without taking his eyes from the piles of glistening curios, he removed the stopper from the brandy bottle on the nearby liquor stand and poured a generous helping into the snifter cupped in his palm. He plucked the cigar from his mouth with an absurd flourish, lifted the snifter, savored the aroma, then took a delicate sip.

Smiling, he shifted his attention to his cigar and took a short puff before setting it gently down on the old-fashioned standing ashtray on the other side of the chair. Slowly, imperceptibly at first, his broad smile dissolved into a puzzled frown. He was tired -- God, he was tired. It must be his age, he thought. Images from better times – at least what he remembered as better times – fought for his attention. Blurry snapshots of his rebellious teenage daughter Sara, then of his long dead wife, flashed through his head, battling to displace the inanimate fortune set before him. His vision blurred.

It had to be around noon. The sun was high in the sky, a blinding ball of fire that leached most of the blue from the heavens. Nunzio was staring stupidly behind him down the road he'd come. There were a few skeletal trees standing here and there on either side of the rutted lane, quivering, flaking in the warm breeze, on the verge of becoming cascading ash. He was aware there were denuded places like this in Sicily, godforsaken places, but he could never recall visiting anything quite so barren. He knew he had to be near Etna, he just wasn't sure of the exact location. The soil was hardly soil at all, but a rocky volcanic brown and black crust with occasional sandy patches.

There was grit between his teeth, and he felt like there was gravel in his mouth. He turned back around and saw what seemed to be Sara up ahead. Except she wasn't a 25-year-old anymore but a small child. There was a thin man dressed all in black following the girl, poised midway between her and Nunzio.

Nunzio still wore his puzzled half frown.

"Papa! C'mon, you're too slow." Sara's voice calling out to him was ineffably sweet. The delicious sound of her words made tears come.

The man impatiently turned for a brief second, and Nunzio was surprised he hadn't recognized him before because it was Carmine, his right hand.

"Carmine, get her to slow down. She's getting too far ahead."

Once more, Carmine twisted his head to look at Nunzio, and Nunzio was startled by his expression. The young man's smile was leering, demonic.

Sara became smaller in the distance. Suddenly Nunzio stumbled on a rock, and he reflexively peered down at his shuffling feet. When he rose again, the sun hit him like a sledgehammer, the heat making his stomach seize up and his heart skip a beat. As his vision cleared, he realized there was something just beyond Sara he had somehow, unfathomably, missed. An ancient villa with an enclosed garden and courtyard loomed.

Nunzio panicked. "Sara, wait! Wait for me!"

Carmine had disappeared, and Sara was about to traipse through the open gate. Nunzio knew all at once that it was the abode of Don Fabrizi, his Godfather.

"Sara, wait! Don't bother Don Fabrizi, he's taking his siesta!"

A loud creaking of splintering boards pierced his ears. He whirled to see a simple, straightback wooden chair sitting beside the path. It very slowly tipped over with a deafening crash. The sound of a little girl shrieking, then crying, welled up from the villa.

"Papa!"

When Nunzio staggered into the shady courtyard, he saw Sara hugging the obscenely fat Don Fabrizi, who sat slumped over in a large wicker throne chair. The Don's face and hands were grey, the color of death, and the thought of elephant skin popped uninvited into Nunzio's flushed imagination. Sara turned, sobbing, a long knife in her right hand and the front of her frilly, powder-blue dress covered in what looked like blood.

Nunzio knelt on rheumatoid knees as Sara raced across the courtyard verandah to embrace him.

"Sara, what have you done!"

"Papa, he…he tried to do things!"

She hugged him around his profusely perspiring neck, and he glanced up at the thunder of running feet.

There were nine of Don Fabrizi's subordinates who had come to a shocked halt a few yards away. Two of the older, middle-aged ones checked out Don Fabrizi's limp, now scarlet corpse. Carmine fought his way to the front of the crowd of rural mafiosi. He gazed with disgust first at Don Fabrizi, then Nunzio and then the weeping child.

"You put her up to this, didn't you? Admit it."

Nunzio caught his breath and stopped short as an overwhelming, tearing pain started below his belt and shoved its way upward through his abdomen and into the middle of his chest. There was the horrible sound of ripping flesh mingled with Sara's ghastly laugh as she gutted him. She yanked herself away and held the bloody blade high above her head.

Nunzio tried to scream but could not. His eyes felt as if they would pop from his head as they stretched wide in a bleary spasm of unbearable suffering. Sara's eyes were wide, too, but gleamed with depraved joy, overflowing with a sickening triumph. Great liquid ropes of thickening blood flooded the baked ground under him.

As darkness fell, there was the crash of breaking glass in the distance.

When Nunzio opened his eyes he was looking at the floor between his legs in front of the oxblood leather chair. A broken brandy snifter lay on the cold stone floor. The brandy looked uncomfortably like blood.

He sank back into the cushion, rubbed his sweating face with both hands and desperately tried to wake up. He felt haggard and old, haunted by some unknown, uninvited presence.

4

JFK was busy and, even though it was 7:30 in the evening, the late August sun still shone brightly through the smeary glass of the huge oblong window by the terminal's escalators.

Yuen, an Asian man in his late thirties, impeccably dressed in a three-piece grey suit, with an eyepatch on the right side of his face and a mane of shaggy black hair, stepped onto the down escalator. His one icy-green cat eye squinted against the blinding glare, scanning the milling crowds with cold precision.

He'd been to America many times since the fall of Saigon, but only to the west coast – Seattle, San Francisco and Los Angeles. New York was something new to him. He could already tell he didn't care for it. He'd been facilitating the smooth transition of gargantuan shipments of heroin for the Triads for over ten years. His dead Chinese father's relatives had folded him into the organization with an uncharacteristic warmth and enthusiasm. It hadn't bothered them that he'd been in the Viet Cong. When he had hit Macao in 1977, disillusioned with Ho Chi Minh and the efforts to rebuild his dead Vietnamese mother's shattered homeland, his uncles had instinctively known all illusions about political solutions for humanity's problems had vaporized from his brain. He had been dead inside where those kinds of ideals had been. Family had been all that was left, and his legendary reputation had preceded him. The fact that he'd already been moving drugs through Cambodia to help finance the Cong had impressed them. When he had come to them, and they had learned the details of his apprenticeship in an efficient, though smaller, smuggling operation, they had jumped at the chance to add his connections and ruthless expertise to their well-oiled machine.

In the back of his mind, he knew that probably at least one of the two men he wanted dead was living in what these fools called the Big Apple. The man who had helped drag his sister, Loan, down into the sewers of Saigon, who had put her in jeopardy so that another lunatic American could kill her. She had stupidly called him her true love. What was his name? Sometimes when his cold desire for vengeance would surge up, the momentary white heat of emotion would erase the man's face and identity from his memory. It was a strange name, even for an American. Milo – that was it. How could he ever forget it? And the other one, Dave Hendricks, who had worked for the CIA, the one who had framed him – Loan's own brother – without a second thought for *her murder* and the death of her killer, the crazy MP cuckold. The fire in his head flamed a frigid blue as he calmed. The evil degradation those two men, as well as so many other American soldiers, had heaped on his poor sister knotted his stomach. The GIs had called her Lucky, a profane bastardization of her name's true meaning, a gross word from a diseased vernacular of uniformed morons. But she had taken part in her own destruction. She had polluted herself with the same poison he was now profiting from. The thought brought him back to why he was there – business.

He saw the three Italian-American men by the baggage claim conveyor belt when he was halfway down the escalator. The one about his age dressed all in black with the dark-blue tie and the calm demeanor was Carmine. He'd met him before in Hong Kong. The tall, overweight middle-aged man and the one who looked like a gawky blond teenager, he could only guess their names.

Carmine obviously spotted him as well and strode purposefully forward to greet him with a smile that exposed yellow teeth. Yuen allowed himself a barely perceptible grin as Carmine took his right hand and pumped it the second he stepped off the escalator.

"Yuen, you look great. Customs go okay? Are you tired? Hungry?"

Yuen only looked at him. Growing uneasy, Carmine introduced his companions.

"These are two of my most trusted men, Rizzo and Anatoli."

Yuen gave them a slight nod, and the two awkwardly responded in kind. Beads of sweat were starting to break out on the usually cold-blooded Carmine's forehead.

"Well, hell, let's get your bags and get out of here, get you over to your hotel."

Yuen raised his briefcase. "This is all I have brought with me. My associates sent my luggage ahead. It is already in my suite."

Carmine looked disappointed, but quickly disguised the flash of uncertainty. His mouth spread into a wide smile again.

"Then let's get the hell out of this zoo!"

Yuen followed beside Carmen as the other two fell behind them.

It was a beautiful Monday morning in lower Manhattan. The August heat had disappeared a couple of hours before dawn and, at 10 AM, it was still more like a spring day than anything else seen so far that summer. There was a gentle, whispering breeze from the direction of the waterfront, and the sky was pure blue, not smog yellow.

Jack Arabella sat in the passenger seat of the car as his wife Anne drove. He absent-mindedly ran his fingers through his thinning hair as he went through the open paper box of manuscript on his lap. He glanced over at her for a second and was caught, as he so often was, by her still astonishing beauty. How had he ever been so fortunate? To know and be married to not only a loving woman, but a beautiful one and, as far as he was concerned, a good one. Although they had eventually come around, his mother and father's initial coolness toward her because she was black still rankled. They were on good terms again, but something had changed between him and his parents that could never be changed back. Being with Anne, he couldn't have cared less what they felt – she was his family now.

"So, honey, how long are you going to be at the Exchange? The usual?"

Anne tilted her head slightly toward him, exasperated. "Till the trading stops at 4. " She grimaced. "You haven't been listening to a word I've said."

Puzzled, Jack turned to stare out the windshield, then back at the papers.

"That's not true. You were talking about Milo."

"Jack, stop going through your manuscript for a minute and look at me."

He sighed, straightened the stack of papers in its box and replaced the cardboard cover.

Anne tried not to laugh. "Goddamn it, don't smile at me like that."

"Okay, go ahead. Finish your thought. Tell me again why you're worried that I'm hanging out too much with Milo."

"That's just it, it's not Milo. I love Milo, even though he'll never change. But he's hanging out with Dave 50% of the time, and Dave is no damn good. Not only that, he's dangerous."

Anne pulled the car over into a loading zone in front of Arcane Encounter, the bohemian bookstore where Jack worked.

"Honey –"

"Don't even, Jack. I know exactly what you're going to say. That Dave is harmless."

"No, I wasn't going to say that. I don't think he's harmless. But he's also not in the League of Super-Villains. Besides you know 50% is an exaggeration."

"What's with Dave, anyway? What's he doing hanging out with penniless Milo? Wasn't he supposed to be some big shot in American intelligence in Vietnam?"

Jack gazed back out the windshield, then at the other side of the street.

"He drank too much and was wrapped too tight. They let him go in 1980. God knows what he does now."

Suddenly, there was a knock on Anne's window, and they both swiveled their heads in that direction. It was Milo, bending over, staring in at them with a shit-eating grin. Anne rolled down the glass, and Milo immediately stuck in his head to buss her on the lips.

"Hi, gorgeous."

She laughed, shy and embarrassed. "Stop!"

Her fresh youth rushed back on them unexpectedly, achingly reminding Jack of what she had been like in high school. Making eye contact with Milo for a split second, he could tell the same memories were welling up.

Milo playfully gestured at Jack. "What're you doing with this baggage?"

Jack blushed and sheepishly smiled. "Hey, man, you're flirting with my wife."

"Jesus, how'd you ever pull a girl like this?"

"Look you two, I don't have time for this adolescent behavior. Some of us have real jobs."

Milo straightened. "Ooh, that hurts! She's talking about you, Jack!"

"I'm talking about both of you good-for-nothings. I've got to get going."

Jack leaned over and kissed her. "Right, baby."

He got out with his manuscript in both hands, kicked closed the door, then leaned in to talk to her through the window.

"You're giving me a look like I've forgotten something…"

"Don't forget there's a deadline on those revisions. You've got to get it over to your publisher today."

Jack smiled. "I know. I'll remember. Love you."

Anne softened, grinned and blew him a kiss. He straightened as she pulled away from the curb. Jack and Milo were left standing, staring at each other over the empty space. A passing car honked, and Jack jumped, looking at the motorist with disgust. He joined Milo on the sidewalk.

"Your wife a little uptight?"

Jack ignored the remark. "What-the-hell are you doing up so early?"

"You know me. I can't sleep half the time anyway."

They walked toward the bookstore.

"I think sometimes she's still in love with you."

Milo stopped, surprised. "Man, don't kid yourself. She married you. She knew I wasn't the right guy. And she wasn't right for me, either. I mean, I love Anne, but look at her, for Christ's sake. She's a stockbroker!"

"All the same, you broke her heart. Coming back from Nam and going crazy with the drugs."

Milo was on the verge of losing his patience.

"That's old news. Do I have to listen to this shit again? Besides things were fucked up between us before I ever went in the army. I was out of school for four years before they shanghaied me in. Four years where she went to college, and I didn't." Jack just looked at him, and it was enough to set Milo off. "Goddamn it. If you keep it up, I'm not going to even tell you the favor I was going to ask you."

"I'm sorry."

They stepped into the chaotic shop, and a little bell rang, knocked by the top of the door.

"Don't fool yourself, Jack. You're her kind of guy. Romantic. Thoughtful all the time. Super-intelligent. Jesus, you're a goddamn authority on 19th-century French poetry, and you're going to have a book published next year."

"But her parents hate me even more than they did you."

"So what. Don't take it personally. You were just the second white guy in a row to go out with her, that's what all that's about."

An elderly lady in thick glasses popped her head out of her book, annoyed. She gave them a disapproving stare. Jason, the gay, fiftyish, hippie proprietor, stood up from his stool behind the counter and glared.

At the opposite end of the store, Yuen poked his head around a bookcase and almost immediately resumed perusing the antique volume in his hands. Suddenly, there was a sixth sense that sent chills up his back. Slowly raising his eyes, he recognized Milo.

Jack was embarrassed at the attention they seemed to be attracting, but Milo was oblivious.

"I better talk to you later."

Milo followed Jack's line of vision, surveying the store. He frowned, then fidgeted so he was facing out the huge glass window. He gazed past Jack's shoulder into the street and lowered his voice.

"Look, don't sweat the small stuff. They don't both hate you, do they?"

Jack remembered they were talking about Anne's parents.

"Anne's mother loves you now, doesn't she?"

Jack begrudgingly smiled. "Well…"

"Yeah, I'm right. So what if her dad still won't be alone in the same room with you. He's one hard-headed son-of-a-bitch."

"Yeah, yeah…I'll see you later."

Milo nodded and started to leave, but Jack grabbed him.

"What was the favor?"

Milo smiled. "It's not important. Later."

Then he was out the door, walking briskly across the street between passing cars.

Yuen lowered the book, watching as Milo disappeared. The last time he'd seen him was in Saigon, skulking out of that alley below Loan's room with blood dripping down his arm. The second he'd spotted Milo back then, an icy shiver had gone through him like a cold knife. The MPs had almost simultaneously screeched to a halt in front of the building, and Dave had quickly come out to meet them. Yuen had tried to get as close as he could, angling to shield himself from view behind the few bystanders starting to cluster around. He had caught Dave in mid-sentence.

" – a big bloody mess. Two bodies – a bar owner named Lucky and one of ours. MP named Jerry Adamson."

One MP had whistled and the other had gasped in a shocked whisper, "Jerry!"

"Yup. Lucky was his girl. Some of the locals, who I agree with, think it was her brother -- "

Yuen's face had flushed with anger, and he had edged back through the growing crowd. Dave had spotted him, and they'd locked stares, but he had made no move to alert the two MPs.

"His name's Yuen. Apparently, he wasn't happy about his sis dating a GI."

Yuen had headed north that very afternoon. He had long hated the American presence there, the vulgar soldiers with their corrupt, profligate ways. But as far as taking sides, he had been on the fence. Loan's death and his need to flee had pushed him over the edge.

Jack moved behind the counter. Jason made room for him, frowning petulantly, but didn't utter a word. A phone rang somewhere in the depths of the bookcases, and Jason disappeared to answer it.

Yuen approached Jack with his book.

"How much?"

Jack took the handsomely bound volume from him.

"Mirbeau. In the original French. I love this book, but I've only read it in English. Can you read French?"

"Yes. I learned it as a child, at the same time as I learned my native language."

"Don't tell me, Vietnamese, right?"

Yuen nodded, faintly grinning. "Yes, the French had an iron grip on us in the fifties when I was a child. They were pigs, the ones that were there in my country. But France has many great writers."

"Where'd you learn English?"

"From my father and my sister. Then much later, American GIs. More pigs." He saw Jack's expression. "Not all, some were okay."

"Yeah. That must've been rough."

"I lost many people." He looked at the book. "Tell me, I'm curious. What does someone like you see in a book like this."

Jack smiled, slightly insulted. "What do you mean someone like me?"

Yuen grinned back. "You just don't seem the type of person that would appreciate such a dark vision of life."

Jack blushed. "I don't know. I love Mirbeau, Lautreamont, Baudelaire, Rimbaud. They all had this hellish vision, this idea – it's hard to explain, but they all opened up a window on what it's like to be caught in the middle between the savage and the spiritual…"

"Go on, I'm listening."

"No. No, I can tell I'm starting to sound pretentious."

"Not at all."

"What about you? What do you get out of a book like *Torture Garden*?"

"Mirbeau had a keen insight into the Asian world's capacity for cold-blooded cruelty. And how decadent European foreigners could feed off of it, like vampires. A symbiotic relationship driving each other to ever more outrageous extremes."

They were both silent for a few seconds.

"My name is Yuen." He extended his hand, and Jack took it warmly in his.

"Jack. Jack Arabella."

"Tell me, Jack, " Yuen turned slightly to face the door, "The man you were just talking to, the one you came in with who just left. He looks familiar."

"Yeah, my friend, Milo. He was over there in Saigon in the early seventies. Maybe you met him."

"Maybe."

5

Marie Neri shifted in the hard, molded plastic shell of her chair in the crowded waiting room. The warren of cubicles and mini-offices in Child Protective Services gave off a strange odor, an acrid mingling of disinfectant, baby vomit and, even though there were No Smoking signs posted everywhere, burnt cigarettes. She nervously squirmed, her ass sore from the unyielding surface. Staring off into space, she absent-mindedly pulled out her own pack, then just as quickly put them back when she realized what she was doing.

Marie felt haggard. Even though men still often told her how good she looked, she feared she must come across at least ten years older than her age of 31.

Her mind wandered back two years – the bottoming out.

The humid night air had been stifling, with not even a hint of breeze coming in from the ocean. She had smoked some meth and some smack, and had finished it off with a raw, full pint of generic supermarket vodka.

She stumbled off the rickety wooden wharf onto the sand, then paused, looking down the shore and out to sea. She knew it was a beach in New Jersey, she just couldn't remember which one. Her flaky drunken date was long gone, the casualty of a petulant disagreement at the carnival a quarter of a mile back.

She could not stand her life any longer.

She knew her face was tear-streaked and, for the first time, she realized that the front of her blouse was torn. She wiped at her mascara-stained cheeks and let out a despairing sob.

There had been something threateningly oppressive about the sky, dark-purple thunderclouds hanging low against the vast expanse of space that had startled her with what she imagined to be the conscious malice of a twisted god. They seemed to be sinking lower toward the water, growing larger all the time, blotting out the twinkling diamonds of stars shimmering in the blackness. Moving into the water, she lunged drunkenly, her bare feet trying to find purchase in the sucking, swirling sand. Once she was out to waist level, something made her turn around to look at the shore.

Frightened Rimi, her baby, toddled after her and suddenly stopped at the water's edge. How could she have given in to the impulse to snuff herself and forgotten Rimi?

"Rimi!"

She awkwardly tripped through the surf, then finally collapsed next to the child, grabbing at the scared little girl just as Rimi was tossed on her backside by an incoming wave. Marie clumsily fumbled, lashing out at her now wet mane of dirty-blonde hair, brushing it from her eyes as she barely regained her feet and swept the baby up out of the water. Terrified by the chaos and her mother's fear, Rimi began to wail.

"Oh, honey. No, don't be following me. Don't ever follow me like that!"

"Neri…Marie Neri?"

Marie came out of her reverie and looked up.

"I do have the right person –?"

A slightly overweight black woman in her mid-forties was staring at her.

"You are Marie Neri...right?"

Marie stood and walked over to the woman.

The caseworker sighed. "Come on in."

She led the way into her cramped office, then edged around the side of her barely accessible desk surrounded by stacks of manila folders and sat down. Once settled, she noticed that Marie was still awkwardly standing in the open doorway.

"Go ahead and sit down, honey, I'm not gonna bite you. And shut that door."

Marie timidly stepped inside, spotted a chair, grabbed it and pulled it up close to the desk.

"What's your story right now?"

Marie gave her a puzzled look as she slowly sank down on the hard surface.

"Your status, sweetheart. Refresh my memory… " The woman opened up a file and started to page through it. "You're still in sober living, right? For at least another three months?"

Marie inched forward. "It's more like another 45 days or so. I'm halfway through the three months."

"Then probation?"

"Yes."

The woman reached down below her desk to her purse and came back up with a cigarette.

"Well, I should tell you – Hey, you can smoke if you want. We're not supposed to, but they're not paying me enough to make me wait for my break."

Marie took out a cigarette, too, but began immediately rummaging through her purse for her lighter. The caseworker leaned over, lit Marie's cigarette, then her own.

"I should tell you, Marie, it doesn't look great right now. Your mother is contesting your petition for custody." She stopped, noticing Marie's crestfallen expression. "I know. I understand you've hinted around about your stepfather and things he's – how should I put it? – capable of? Don't worry, it doesn't look good for your mother, either. At the moment, anyway." The woman took a long drag, then let out a cloud of smoke. "But as far as you go, it's really too soon for you to think about being a mother again. You need to be clean and stay that way. You need to get a job, when they'll let you. You'll be doing what your little girl is doing...baby steps."

Marie didn't say anything, just stared down at her knees. Absentmindedly, she took a puff on her cigarette.

"What happened with you anyway, honey? You started college pretty late but you were doing well your first couple of years. Then, bang! The last four have been downhill – dropping out, getting pregnant, getting strung out."

Marie looked up at her. "I'm not sure what happened. One day everything seemed okay. I was out there, living. Things were scary, but I was getting by, then suddenly – I don't know. I really don't know what happened. I was drinking. I knew some friends who got high, and I did a little taste to take the pressure off – "

"Then the next thing you know you're turning tricks down on

Avenue A, attempting suicide and ending up here."

Marie averted her eyes, staring into space.

"Don't get me wrong. I'm not trying to make you feel bad. I'm sure you do a good enough job of that on your own." She paused, closing the file. "Listen, honey, just keep your nose clean. Do what they tell you. Do what their program says – what is it? Take one day at a time?"

Marie nodded.

"Before you know it, you'll be back here, and things will be working out. You'll have your little girl back. That is, if you don't fuck things up."

Marie stood and reached out her hand.

The woman smiled as she firmly grasped Marie's palm. "My name's Aggie. Call me if you really need to talk, okay?"

Marie smiled back. "Thanks for being honest with me. And for not being an asshole."

Marie automatically looked up at the sky when she came out of the building. It had become overcast while she was inside, but the heat was still rising off the street in humid waves. Sweat beaded up on her face and arms within seconds.

Throngs of people, with all their attendant odors, surrounded her on the sidewalk, sidestepping to get around her. Realizing she was in the way, she backed up against the wall of the building. She felt overwhelmed.

6

The large coffee urn wasn't particularly heavy, but it was ungainly, and carrying it over eight blocks from where he had picked it up was a pain in the ass. Milo shifted from lugging it by the handles to hugging the ancient silver canister to his chest, all the while navigating to avoid oblivious people who were coming at him on the sidewalk from the opposite direction. The cigarette dangling from his lips suddenly let go of its built-up ash, and a cinder flew into his eye. He skillfully dodged a fat, hard-charging merchant with a bundle of dresses slung over his shoulder, then propped the coffee maker against the grimy wall of a condemned delicatessen, using his wrist to rub his tearing eyelid and clear his vision. He looked down the street. Only another half block.

Father Culkin stood beneath the hand-painted sign that read Green Pastures, greeting the strange variety of people showing up for the AA meeting in the storefront rehab. It was a blue-collar Brooklyn neighborhood in a strange limbo perched between Bed-Stuy and Park Slope, with its share of the homeless. But the working class and down-trodden weren't the only ones breezing through the open door. A few serene-looking businessmen, with their ties loosened or missing altogether, often showed up for the late-afternoon meeting.

What had played out the year before at St. Margaret's in lower Manhattan ran through Milo's mind like an old movie. Culkin had been kicked out of the parish by the Monsignor and was suspended from his priestly duties pending review from the Bishop. His personality was outgoing and giving, but he also was afflicted with a chip on his shoulder, the roots of which stemmed from a deeply troubled childhood. Some parishioners had protested that Aloysius was discriminating against the young priest because he was black and a social activist. But Milo knew, as Culkin did deep down inside himself, that the banishment was the direct result of his uncontrollable temper.

Culkin's smile evaporated when he saw Milo.

"Sorry. Elmo couldn't make it. I had to go by his place to pick up the coffeemaker."

"I told him he wasn't supposed to take it home. It's supposed to stay here on the premises." Culkin plucked Milo's cigarette from his mouth and flicked it into the street. "Go on, get in there. The girl who's supposed to make the coffee is waiting."

Milo made a beeline through the 30 or so people who congregated in the main room, many of them setting up folding chairs. He nodded at greetings shouted in his direction as he elbowed his way to the counter that gave way to the kitchen. A sad-looking, pretty girl he hadn't seen before was reaching across the polished linoleum bartop, setting out a plate of store-bought cookies. She spotted him and seemed to brighten.

As he rounded the open door, Marie met him, taking the coffeemaker from his hands with a smile.

"Thank God you got here. Father Culkin was about to have a heart attack."

Milo leaned against the sink, watching, as she began filling it with water, then put in the filter and the coffee. She glanced up and smiled as she hurriedly finished. But when she tried to lift it again, it had grown too heavy. Milo winked at her as he picked it out of her hands, moved quickly across the narrow room, set it in place on the countertop and plugged it in.

During the meeting, Marie sat right in the front row, hemmed in on both sides by two slightly older women with graying hair and vaguely hippie attire. Milo took his usual place standing in the back, propping himself up on the storefront's high windowsill. The meeting's speaker was a blocky, bullnecked man in his sixties with a bristling white shock of crewcut hair – a retired cop who'd busted him ten years before on a paraphernalia beef on 42nd Street. It was a strange fucking world. His pitch sported a bizarre mélange of Boston and Brooklyn accents.

"What do I do now, now that I'm not draining gallons of rotgut vodka, now that I'm not hijacking dope from street hookers? I just try to take things as they come. I don't try to get everything accomplished at once. You can't stay sober if you're in a big hurry. You can't be all in the future or all in the past. You have to stay in the here and now… "

When it was over, and people started to finally drift off from post-meeting conversations, Marie decided to have another cigarette. She was trying to cut down, but the feeling of being so newly clean was getting to her. Standing on the curb outside, with the damn thing already in her mouth, she once again couldn't find the lighter in her purse. Then Milo was there beside her, pulling some matches from his shirt and striking a flame. She leaned over, touched the end of it to the fire and inhaled deeply.

"Marie, right?"

She exhaled the smoke and beamed. "Yeah."

He stuck out his hand, and she shook it. "Milo."

"Wow, what a name."

"It's actually not my original name. People started calling me Milo in high school, and it carried over to Nam. It's from the character in a book...you know, *Catch 22*?"

"I've heard of it…haven't read it, though. Why'd they call you that?"

"Because the guy in the book was always on the hustle. Always trying to make a fast buck behind the scenes. Black market, things like that."

Marie raised her eyebrows.

Milo laughed softly. "I was nowhere near as bad as the guy in the book. I did stuff, but I was a small-timer."

"And what's your real name?"

"Real?" His smile broadened. "Milo's my real name now. When I got back from Nam, everybody who knew me from before, everybody here in Brooklyn, even my mom, was calling me that."

"How long were you in Vietnam?"

"About two years, right near the end. I left when Saigon fell."

Marie looked down the street at the smog-shrouded sun that was getting ready to set. "My brother died over there."

A lull in the traffic punctuated an uncomfortable silence. They were both distracted by the blaring of a car horn almost directly across the street. A blood-red Lincoln Continental convertible was double-parked, and Milo immediately recognized the fat mobster Rizzo behind the wheel. His immediate superior, underboss Carmine, was next to him, his head resting lazily on the top of the passenger seat. He was staring into the clear sky, his left arm draped over the upholstery as his other hand languidly angled a cigarette up to his thin, cruel lips. He blew smoke rings dreamily into the cooling evening air.

A young man – Milo thought his name might be Anatoli – came out of the brownstone, followed by Mal, a tall black man who was the neighborhood drug dealer.

“C’mon, already! Jeezus H. fucking Christ!” Rizzo smacked his forehead in exasperation.

“Coming!”

Anatoli childishly skipped down the steps while Mal remained at the top of the stoop, sullenly watching as the kid jumped in the rear seat, and the mobsters careened off. Mal started to turn, but stopped as he caught sight of Marie and Milo staring at him. He smirked nastily, shook his head in disgust, then disappeared inside the tenement.

“You know him?”

“Unfortunately. Neighborhood dealer. Name’s Mal. As you can see, he has to go to the mob for his stuff.”

“Those guys in the car were mob?”

Milo smiled indulgently at her sweet naivete. “Where’re you from?”

Marie laughed, coloring slightly. “I’m originally from upstate, a little place called Suffern. You probably never heard of it.”

“I’ve heard of it.” Milo paused, looking up and down the block. “What’re you doing now, Marie? You want to get a bite to eat?”

She grimaced, dropped the butt and ground it out beneath one heel. “I’d love to. But I can’t. I’ve got to get back to the sober living house.” She pointed down the street. “It’s three blocks down and a block over, that way. I shouldn’t even be talking to you. Technically, I’m not supposed to be fraternizing with the opposite sex for the first 90 days, which I’m only halfway through.”

“Yeah, that place. They’re pretty strict over there. Well… maybe another time.”

“I’d like that.” She looked at him for a brief second, then suddenly turned and was off. After a few steps, she turned around, but continued on, walking backwards.

“I’m here every day, though. You know, for the afternoon meeting.”

Milo leaned against the street lamp, smiled, nodded and waved.

The deepening dusk on 69th and Colonial put the Fiorile Restaurant sign in deep shadow.

Carmine became distracted from his conversation with Rizzo, Anatoli, Gino and Farini as night slowly crept into the neighborhood. He looked up from the sidewalk and saw the timer still wasn't working. The goddamn neon outlining the name Fiorile hadn't clicked on. Suddenly he got a dig in his ribs from Rizzo, who was wagging his head toward the street. Mal's beat-up, chocolate-colored Oldsmobile with the white hardtop was double-parked in the middle of the narrow thoroughfare. Carmine nervously scanned the block, then walked up to the driver's side. Rizzo glanced at the others, shaking his massive pork-barrel head in revulsion. Carmine was keeping his voice down so they couldn't hear what was said, but you could tell he was pissed off, by the way his arms were pumping and waving. Abruptly Mal peeled out, tires squealing and exhaust pipe belching grey smoke.

After watching Mal disappear around the corner, Carmine stared across the street. Two Feds, O'Reilly and Mullen, were standing in plain sight, still wearing their sunglasses and deadpan expressions, each casually sipping coffee from styrofoam cups.

Carmine stoically kept his cool.

"*Carmine!*" It was Rizzo, urgently half-whispering, turned away from the entrance so his profile showed, hooking his thumb behind him. Carmine slowly swiveled his head to see Nunzio standing in the open doorway. Once Nunzo made eye contact, he crooked his finger. He did not look happy. Carmine stepped up on the sidewalk, and Nunzio rolled over with his intimidating gait to meet him, turning him around, pushing him in the small of the back toward the Lincoln Continental parked a few cars down the curb. Gino and the older, grey-haired Farini instinctively held back, but Rizzo and Anatoli started to follow.

Like he had eyes in the back of his head, Nunzio whirled.

"Did I say anything to you two? Did I tell you to come with us?"

The blood drained from their faces. They shrugged their shoulders and contritely shook their heads. Carmine stood behind Nunzio, mortified. He put his hands on his hips and stared down at the sidewalk.

"Damn right I didn't tell you two to tag along! Now get your asses off the street and inside!"

Rizzo and Anatoli were petrified, dumbly looking at Nunzio, then at Carmine.

Nunzio did a double take and exploded afresh. "What're you two scumbags doing looking at *him!* Hunh? I told you to get the fuck inside!" He pointed at the restaurant. "Fucking now!"

The two sweating men stumbled over themselves getting through the door. Nunzio stared after them, then turned to find Carmine in his agitated posture.

"And you, what're you looking so persecuted for? Eh? Get in the fucking car already!" His sixth sense ringing alarm bells, he noticed the smiling Feds across the street. "No, wait a minute. Put up the goddamn top first."

Carmine let his arms fall abjectly to his side, powerless against his boss's wrath. He yanked the top up on the Continental in record time, not once looking at Nunzio. Once done, Nunzio climbed in, and Carmine followed suit.

The car interior was already warming and becoming stuffy.

"I know what you're going to say -- "

Nunzio lashed out and slapped him on the back of the head.

"Oh, we have a goddamn clairvoyant in our midst. You know what I'm gonna say? Then why do I have to fucking say it? Didn't I tell you a hundred times about having him and his kind come to this neighborhood? Even if I didn't care about it setting a goddamn precedent, making them think it's okay for them to show their black asses here on our turf, even if I didn't give a good fucking goddamn about that, I wouldn't want them here talking to us 'cause it tells everyone on the block with half a brain we're working with them. Including those two goddamn Feds who have next to no brains at all."

Carmine was ashen.

"Understood?"

Carmine nodded. He tried to remain calm, but knew his voice was awkwardly defensive. "I just tore him a new asshole right now, about him coming by. You don't know how many – "

"Did I say you could talk? I'm not finished. You know we've got those fucking Justice Department pricks crawling up our asses. You see 'em all the time. They're watching us right now! Why the hell do you think I made you put up the top? I was almost going to take you into the office, but wasn't sure it was wise. We haven't swept for bugs in a couple of days." Nunzio paused, staring out the windshield, exasperated. Carmine could tell the storm was finally subsiding.

He decided to take a chance and grovel. "I'm sorry."

Nunzio pivoted his head, scowled and changed the subject. "How old's that kid you've got with you now? What's'is name? Anatoli?

"Anatoli, yeah. He's eighteen."

"He may be eighteen, but he's younger in the head. I can tell looking at him. He's got the eyes of a fourteen-year-old."

"He's okay. He's Rizzo's cousin."

"A good kid?"

Carmine nodded.

Nunzio's voice had assumed a friendlier tone, but there was still gentle admonishment spewing forth.

"I'll take your word for it. But I'll tell you, Carmine, you got to tell this crew to watch it. I know none of 'em are rats. But they gotta remember to watch what they're saying, even inside here at the restaurant. Everyone of 'em likes to hear himself talk." He paused, then smiled. "You eaten?"

Carmine shook his head.

"You probably don't feel much like eating right now. But go on in, have a glass of wine, cool off. Have some supper."

Carmine stared at him.

"Go on." Nunzio dismissed him with a wave of his hand. "Go on, I'll be in in a minute or two."

As Carmine left with his tail between his legs, Nunzio pulled out a cigar.

Rizzo and Anatoli were wedged into a plush booth, devouring plates of spaghetti doused in a heavy marinara sauce.

"So, tell me, who's the one-eyed gook we had to pick up the other day at the airport?"

"Don't let Carmine hear you call him that." Rizzo conspiratorially lowered his voice. "You ever hear of the Golden Triangle?"

Anatoli snickered like a pre-pubescent boy. "What? You mean some blonde's muffin?"

"No, you dipshit. It's the border area where Cambodia, Laos and Thailand meet. They grow the strongest opium poppies in the world there. Our yellow friend with the eyepatch is a middleman in a pipeline Carmine's trying to set up."

"Opium?"

"No, dunsky. Scag. Smack. Horse. Junk – you know, *heroin!*" He peered over his shoulder to make sure no one was listening. "That guy's a stone killer. Carmine saw him whack five guys at once when he was in Hong Kong a few months ago. The guy didn't even break a sweat, and Carmine practically worships him now. Carmine's asking him to help us track down this guy who's knocking over the dealers."

"Keep your goddamn mouths shut about that. You two know better." Carmine glared down at them. "Move the fuck over." He tousled Anatoli's hair as he slid in. He immediately grabbed the carafe, poured a glass of wine and chugged it.

"Man, he was hot. Did you tell him?"

Carmine was incredulous at how stupid Rizzo could sometimes be. "Are you kidding? How could I tell him that we've had three of our dealers knocked off in as many weeks when he was chewing out my ass 'cause that nigger was stupid enough to show his face."

"In broad daylight yet! What did he say?"

"Do I have to tell you? Isn't it obvious?"

"No, not the boss. I know what he said. What did Mal want?"

Carmine downed another glass. He took a deep breath and gave them both meaningful looks. "He heard about the rip-offs, our three guys eating it. Not to mention what happened to that renegade spic in Harlem. He's scared."

"That big ape motherfucka? Scared?"

Carmine held his tongue. God, Rizzo was annoying the shit out of him today.

"Just let me get my hands on the motherfucker. I wish we knew who the fuck it was."

Carmine softened at Anatoli's teenage machismo.

"Don't worry, kid. We may not know yet. But we will. We will."

7

Dave's loft, though of decent size, was furnished with only a few sticks of furniture. Two rickety wooden chairs, which looked as if they'd passed through numerous second-hand stores, were aligned haphazardly with a dirty, paint-splattered mahogany table. Dave was hunched over the scratched-up top, going through his mail. He snorted in disgust, wrapped a rubber band around the pile and tossed it on his sleeping bag.

A metallic clanking from somewhere down below startled him. The address was not far from Boston and 173rd in the Bronx. It wasn't quite the burned-out ruins the blocks had been in the early 1980s, but it was still pretty bad. He was the only tenant in what had previously been a hybrid office industrial building, and he had the freight elevator stationed on his floor. Since the apathetic owner was actually toying with the idea of remodeling and had completely destroyed the stairs and the fire escapes, it was the only way left now to enter his apartment. Spooked, he pushed away from the table, stood and sauntered casually over to the elevator gate. He put his greasy head up against the edge of the shaft, his eyes shifting, his ears pressed lovingly to metal and zeroing in along one span of the five-story-high, iron girder cage…nothing.

Parked at the table once more, he stared out the open window before him, seeing, yet not seeing the grimy, overcast horizon pierced by the broken battlements of sagging tenements. He closed his eyes, stroked his several days' growth of beard and then meticulously dived into the pieces of his Browning 9mm scattered on the sticky wood. Despite the onset of arthritis, his fingers were nimble, and he had the gun assembled within a shockingly quick minute.

Dave crouched low on the rotting rooftop. Casually, surreptitiously, he poked his head over the raised brick and mortar border running along the edge. It was a bit southeast of where he lived, not too far from Charlotte Street, but many street signs below were missing, so he wasn't positive of the actual intersection. Shit, he thought, this neighborhood makes mine look like Park Avenue. The building next door was also vacant, but a hub of illicit activity. A line of misbegotten addicts of all shapes, sizes and colors sweated in line on the sidewalk of the condemned slum, fidgeting impatiently, waiting for their turn up the stairs to purchase their drug of choice. Every time Dave saw people lined up like that, it took him back. Lines of refugees standing outside the American compound in Saigon.

There was that one afternoon he'd been on the sidewalk beyond the fence with a woman he knew, a friend of a friend whom he'd agreed to help, to make sure she got through the gate and onto one of the last choppers going to the airfield. He'd been standing a few feet from her, turned away to buy a newspaper when there had been a white starburst of light, followed a second later by an earsplitting concussion. Somehow, he'd been miraculously untouched and only momentarily deafened. When he'd turned around, there were still lines of people stretched as far as his eyes could see, but the ones in his immediate vicinity were just bottom halves – legs and half torsos – with the rest of their bodies missing. A red mist was slowly settling over pulps of bloody flesh caked on the iron fence and the concrete walls and walk. And the woman acquaintance he'd been standing next to with the baby in her arms was gone – at least as far as he could see. Apparently, he'd been standing there for a good ten minutes while the dust and gore settled, oblivious to the screams and chaos, the grotesque upright limbs and groins standing ruptured like huge fleshy flowers, the panicking lined-up refugees and the shouting soldiers. At last, a baby-faced GI and someone he later recognized as Milo had come out of the compound and gently pulled him back, coaxing him into the yard, then across it through the throngs of jostling, frightened people, into the shelter of the building.

Once inside, Milo had sat him down on the bottom step of a

rear exit staircase and had carefully begun wiping off the bloody corpse tissue from his sticky skin. At one point, Milo had drawn in his breath, sickened and horrified, and it had snapped Dave out of his shock long enough to look down to where Milo was staring. The perfectly formed outer layer of the woman's baby's face was plastered like a grotesque 3-D tattoo on his forearm. One squashed eyeball still hung from a flattened socket. It had taken Dave a good minute to realize exactly what it was, and when he'd raised his eyes to look into Milo's, he had suddenly broken down. It was the only time since he was a kid he could remember crying. And he recalled little else after that. It was strange that it had gotten to him. He'd seen so much degrading, dehumanizing violence. He'd seen and heard nightmarish things during interrogations and in the bush. He'd done coldblooded, bestial things himself. He'd seen dead children before, in immolated villages. Milo hadn't known all the details of what Dave had seen and had done, but he had known enough – known enough that the perfectly formed infant's face emblazoned on Dave's arm had been the straw that broke the camel's back.

Dave had learned later that the Cong who had thrown the bomb had been trying to kill *him*, and the one reason why he had remained amongst the living was a stroke of absurd, blind luck. A food vendor's cart had come between him and the woman and her baby, the bomb landing on her other side. The metal of the cart had somehow deflected the blast like a reflective funnel toward her and the people behind her.

Dave thought about Milo. He held feelings for his friend he held for no other person on earth. Sometimes he wondered if he was queer. But they weren't sexual feelings. It was both fraternal and paternal, and very deep. He'd never felt that way about his parents nor any of the women he'd been with – though truth be told, all the women with whom he'd been intimate he considered slopbucket whores.

He felt protective of Milo. Yet that day, Milo had been the caregiver and had shown an unconditional compassion and understaning that had only grown since they'd returned stateside. Particularly since Milo had gotten sober after his near-fatal coma, the result of a fractured, head-busting jewel of a speedball. At the time, the doctors had worried he might have suffered brain damage. He had come out of it after three days, comparatively okay, although occasionally suffering hallucinations. Dave thought Milo must have been having one of those spells when he was sitting on the curb in front of St. Margaret's that recent afternoon.

A faint blur of motion on the periphery of his vision galvanized him into action. One of the dealer's lookouts on the roof next door had spotted him. Dave calmly raised his 9mm with silencer, steadied it on his left forearm and put a whispery *phhtt!* of lead between the frizzy-haired Puerto Rican teenager's eyes. The body collapsed with a dull thwack. He slipped the gun back in his camouflage jacket as he glanced below to see if anyone on the sidewalk had noticed.

He swiveled his head, scouting for the other lookouts. There was one on either end of the alley, but their attention was focused outward toward the respective streets.

Dave had built a bridge out of pieces of nailed-together plywood two days previous, leaving it on the shabby tarpaper, and he now quickly slid one end of it across to perch on the edge of the opposite building's roof. Checking the lookouts again, he saw that they hadn't noticed a thing. The swarming bustle of jonesing humanity held the nearest man's attention while the other was too far away and distracted, lighting a cigarette. Dave creepy-crawled swiftly across, pulled the bridge over to his new vantage point and glided to the rooftop door.

Entering the interior stairwell as quietly as possible, Dave peered over the sixth-floor landing – which really was nothing but an extra-wide, extremely dusty thick plank platform equipped with a short ladder to the roof – and withdrew his automatic. By the murmur of voices wafting upward, he could tell he'd deduced right from his previous scouting expeditions. The one lone apartment with the drugs and money, the little brain-frying bodega, was in the belly of the building – probably halfway down on the third floor. He stared beneath him, watching the squared pit in the center of the six floors and the sets of angled steps. He slowly started his climb down.

Sure enough, a bulky muscle-bound guard with a bullet-head stood on the third floor landing with his back to the stairs leading to the upper levels. A hunched-over buyer, a grizzled black man of indeterminate age, murmured to himself as he turned away from the nearest apartment door with the oblong slot cut in the center. He jammed his stuff in the inside pocket of his greased-grey denim jacket and stumbled down the steps. The bullet-headed oaf leaned over the balustrade and motioned for the next customer. Dave glanced at the slot. The small transaction trap was shut, and no one seemed to be peering out. Instinctively knowing the time was right, he quickly, quietly crept up behind the guard, yanked him back by his leather jacket's collar, simultaneously putting a bullet in the back of his skull and swinging him with the momentum down into the shadows of the unlit corridor.

He took bullet-head's place just as a weary-looking Puerto Rican woman came into view on the landing. Dave motioned her over to the dealer's door, then whirled and shot her with an insect-like *phhtt!* as soon as her back was turned. He shoved her body down the hall to land on top of the guard's, now no more to Dave than an awkward bag of dirty laundry. Composing himself in a matter of seconds, he serenely took his place at the entrance and tapped on the trap partition with the gun. As soon as it opened, he stuck the barrel through to rest on the sweaty brow of the man peering out.

"Open or I give you a third eye."

The lock clicked and, when the inner-sanctum opened, Dave rammed his way in, quietly shutting the door.

A scrawny, scared-looking black teenager stood there in his path, visibly quaking. Just beyond, an unshaven, 30-something white man went for the semi-automatic on the cluttered table next to the cash box. Dave coolly shot him. The man fell to the floor, a bullethole leaking blood from his right ear.

Dave and the teenager just stood there for a seeming eternity, staring into each other's souls. The boy's eyes were brimming with tears, but Dave's were cold, steely, devoid of all human compassion. There was the *phhtt!* of the silencer again and then a muffled thud as another body hit the grimy floorboards. Dave kicked the kid's corpse over with his square-toed boot and looked into the impossibly young, ashen, frozen-in-surprise face. Life was trickling out. Dave suddenly saw flames being extinguished all over the world. Countless little tear-drops of fire going out at the slightest breeze. That's what he was – a fireman. Putting out fires wherever he was needed. That's all he was good for, and he was not the kind of man to let his one remaining talent go to waste. The thought made him sigh, but it also galvanized him into ruthless action, plunging him forward towards the open cash box where he grabbed fistfuls of bills, repeatedly jamming them deep into his bottomless camouflage jacket pockets. There had to be at least five grand. Not bad at-fucking-all!

He grabbed another two boxes, one full of microscopic, folded blue cellophane envelopes of smack, another with red ones of rock. He peered through the trap slot to make sure the coast was clear, stuck his gun inside his jacket, then unceremoniously left with nary a glance behind at his gory handiwork. He casually, specifically placed the two open drug boxes equidistant from each other on the landing, then started slowly downstairs.

Dave took on the persona of an excited crackhead as he began to pass buyers lined up on the steps.

"Wow, it's a trip, man! There's two boxes of free dope just sitting there at the top of the steps with no one around!"

A loud murmur gradually welled from the scruffy customers as Dave repeated his message on his descent. By the time he reached the bottom, people were flooding up the stairs, and he stopped to crane his neck to glance at the ascending stampede.

When Dave came out the side door of the building, the panicking guard, unable to stem the flow of addicts, grabbed his arm.

"What-the-fuck's going on!"

Dave gave him a bewildered, heavy-lidded look. "Dunno, man. Some heavy shit."

The guard took off, racing inside. Another two guards jostled him as they flew past into the building.

Dave had to stifle a laugh.

8

The sparkling-clean black town car pulled to the curb in front of the large two-story house on Beverley Road in Brooklyn, not far from the corner of Westminster. A burly fat guy named Gus, who seemed about to burst the seams of his satin jacket and sweat pants, tumbled out of the driver's side, his tree-stump legs catching his torso before it could hit the asphalt. He casually looked back and forth on the block, then made his way to the passenger side, opening the door for his boss.

Nunzio catapulted out, bridling inside at some unspecified offender's transgression, a nebulous, blurry fire of resentment the origin of which he couldn't even really put his finger on himself.

He stared at the upper windows to the right, his daughter Sara's bedroom, stood there transfixed, his upturned face like stone while Gus clumsily vaulted the few steps and unlocked the front door.

'C'mon, boss, it's gettin' cold."

Nunzio came out of his reverie. "What're you talking about? It's gotta be at least 70 degrees."

Gus sheepishly answered, "Well, comparatively speaking…" He pressed himself against the outside wall as Nunzio shoved passed him into the house.

The dark warmth of the foyer opened onto the rich shadows of the living room. The television was on with some stupid teen pop music program running without the sound, but no one was there. Nunzio raised his eyes again, gazing at the ceiling, then up the stairs.

"Want somethin' to eat?"

Distracted, Nunzio didn't look at him, "No, I'll fix something later myself. Go on in and see what's in the fridge if you're hungry."

Gus shrugged and edged by, and Nunzio's feet sank into the plush red pile as he started to climb the carpeted steps.

Even though Sara, Nunzio's daughter, was 25 years old, her bedroom was plastered with the posters of sexy movie stars. The photos were artistic, tasteful, obviously shot by someone good like Avedon, Liebowitz or Bailey and in stark black-and-white. But the room still looked like it belonged to a teenager – though a decidedly hip teenager.

Sara nervously fidgeted in her sexy black lingerie and garter belt, compulsively scrunching up her scrawny but attractive frame as she sat down in front of her make-up mirror. She had pulled on only one of her stockings when there was a knock at the door. She stopped, her happy expression suddenly frozen.

"Malizia?"

Her father's muffled voice trumpeted through the wood. "No, Sara, it's me. Malizia went home."

She shook her head, silently mouthing the word "Shit!" Her long black hair fell in clumps, hiding her aquiline face.

"Can I come in, honey?"

Sara rolled her eyes, then impatiently gave him a sing-songy answer.

"*I'm* dressing, *Daddy*. I'll be *down* in a few *minutes*."

She carefully listened and thought she heard him walk away and start downstairs. When she looked back at herself in the mirror, the snapshot of her long dead boyfriend, Dillon, caught her eye. He hadn't been much, but he hadn't had a mean bone in his body. He hadn't been a gangster, either – a characteristic for which he'd been labeled a fag by her sweet father. Then he'd gone and done something stupid and gotten himself killed playing chicken on the railroad tracks with his drunken friends. The moron.

When Nunzio reached the bottom step, he glimpsed Gus through the open door to the kitchen, sitting at the table and hungrily chowing down. He grimaced at his driver's sloppy manners, then shuffled wearily into the living room, plopping down in his easy chair. Manhandling the TV remote, he switched to the news and turned the volume up until it was a low murmur. Restless and impatient, he compulsively changed channels until he arrived at a WWII documentary that seemed to be chronicling Nazi concentration camps.

He settled there, momentarily comforted for some strange reason, partly from nostalgia for his wartime exploits and his making it back alive. There was also something about seeing those atrocities, such disregard for human dignity and life, on such a massive scale in those factories of death, that seemed to diminish his own culpability in his own personal transgressions. Yes, he had murdered – he didn't like that word; "killed" was a better one – and he had even mercilessly, cruelly tortured rat finks and unprincipled rivals. But he, Nunzio, was a piker, a small-timer compared to the mid-20th century German bureaucracy of wholesale fatality. Besides, some of those greedy hebes undoubtedly deserved what they got. The bald-faced hypocrisy of that idea stung him out of nowhere as he involuntarily remembered Aloysius' guilty conscience about their war booty. He shuddered, then reprimanded himself for being such a sob sister. He did not believe in, nor had he ever surrendered, to self-reflection, asserting it was the province of the weak, even after the sudden death of his wife many years previous.

For some reason, every time he saw Sara now she made him think of his dead spouse. Her name, Andrea, spelled out in big block letters, came into his head, and he had to chase it out. Seeing her name, hearing his own voice call it, stabbed through him like a blade of ice. He shivered. What was it? Sara was starting to look like her more and more every goddamn day.

He remembered when he had first met Andrea so long ago when she was in her early twenties and he in his late thirties. The fact that he'd been connected hadn't fazed her then. She had had uncles and distant cousins who were made men, but no one in her immediate family. Her father had been a grocer who had resisted the call of easy money and, what's more, he hadn't had the backbone for it, even if he had been so inclined. Gradually, though, Andrea's sharp intelligence, her dissecting eye – despite her lack of education – had picked up on some of the more distasteful aspects that went with his "work." She had overheard a very young Carmine discussing the dismemberment and disposal of a no-good rotten stoolie rat's stab-ridden body. She had noticeably cooled toward him after that. She had never specifically brought it up, but he knew she knew. And she knew he knew she knew. It had caused a shame to grow in his heart, a shame for things his peers chided him that he never should be ashamed about. Why the fuck had she had to have been so smart? Why the fuck couldn't she have just insulated herself here at home like all the other wives?

Then there had also been the fact he'd been unfaithful to her many times. She had known that, too. But, hell, it was routine for men like him. He still believed the old ways were best. The woman's province, her limited kingdom, was the house; his was all else that spread itself before him. He was lord of the domain, free to spread his seed wherever he saw fit inside his own family or outside it. The wife's duty was sacred. To keep her mouth shut, to stay at home and hold the family together. She had slowly descended at a sure and steady pace into an alcoholism so acute it had sickened him. No matter what he had tried, nothing had worked. Being kind, being cruel. Slapping and cursing, yelling and beating her blue.

And he had found himself unable to desire her anymore, even if she had still been letting him into her bed. Then a funny thing started happening. Except it wasn't fucking funny at all. The rare time he had still desired her, the whole incident she'd overheard Carmine discussing – with his big goddamn mouth – would be replayed. Thinking of her sexually had made him remember Mac the Hat's body parts, big messy red chunks of flesh being thrown into the bay for shark food by Carmine, Rizzo and Johnny Gusti. The four of them drinking beer after lukewarm beer and laughing uncontrollably as Mac – what was left of Mac – disappeared into the salty black water.

The sound of Sara's feet thumping energetically downstairs made him turn his head.

"Where-the-hell do you think you're going?"

She stopped a few steps from the bottom, a practiced expression of innocent surprise on her face. "To the movies with Cecilia."

"Like that?"

"What!" She looked down at her sexy dress with an exaggeratedly indignant air.

"You don't know?"

Gus, half a sandwich in one hand and a beer in the other, shuffled out of the kitchen and gaped at Sarah.

"You look nice."

"Thanks, Gus." She made a point of regularly flirting with the big lout and smiled shyly. "I'm glad someone thinks so."

"Who asked you! Back in the kitchen!"

Gus shivered under Nunzio's icy eyes and slunk back from whence he'd come.

Nunzio swiveled his head around to Sara, walking a few paces towards her.

"Movies again with Cecilia. This is the second night in a row."

"So what? There's some good shit playing for once!"

"Watch the language! The sisters and your mother and I didn't bring you up to talk like that!"

"You're unbelievable. How dare you bring up Mom! And since when did you ever take stock in what the goddamn sisters said? What a crock of shit!"

Nunzio's face flushed, a hot crimson of anger and guilt.

"You are really pushing your goddamn friggin' luck. I told you to cut the language. I'm your father! You don't talk to me that way, ever. You hear?"

For a long moment they stared each other down, the modulated whisper of the TV the only sound in the room.

Finally, after what seemed an eternity, Sara shrugged. "Okay, I won't go."

Nunzio watched her take a couple of steps back upstairs, then shook his head, mad at himself. "Did I say that?"

Sara stopped. It was the same as always. They'd argue, and she'd finally guilt-trip him enough to relent.

"Go! Go ahead…get outta here."

Sara practically jumped the rest of the way to the bottom and, in one quick, practiced motion, slipped into her long, black leather jacket that was hanging by the front door.

"Thanks, Daddy!"

"It'd be nice if you spent a little more time at home with your old man once in a while."

The door slamming nearly drowned out Sara's jubilant, "Bye!"

Halfway down the stoop, Sara paused, a trancelike poisonous caste clouding her pretty features. "Hypocrite."

She continued in awkward, herky-jerky steps down to the sidewalk and Cecilia's waiting late-model Chevy.

"He give you shit again?"

"What do you think?" Sara shut the passenger door and peered at the house through her window.

Nunzio stood there with the drapes pulled aside, staring at them.

Cecilia stepped on the gas, rubber squealed, and the Chevy peeled down the street.

In the living room, Gus came over to join his boss at the window.

Nunzio didn't look at him, his eyes fixed on Cecilia's disappearing taillights. He muttered through clenched teeth. "She got into Cecilia's car, but she's seeing somebody. I just know it."

"Maybe I should start following her."

"No, no, I don't want to have happen to her what happened with her mother."

Gus didn't understand. "What do you mean?"

"I pushed too hard with her mother. And look what happened."

"You can't blame yourself for that, boss."

Nunzio turned around, staring into space.

"You couldn't have known she was going to get drunk like that and – "

Nunzio pivoted his head just enough to give Gus an arctic stare that froze the blood in his veins. Gus quickly waddled back into the kitchen.

Three blocks away, Cecilia's Chevy slowed to a stop alongside Carmine's scarlet Lincoln Continental convertible. Sara jumped out, waved goodbye to Cecilia as she pulled away, then ran around the front of Carmine's car. He opened the passenger door for her, and she sailed into the front seat. They immediately locked lips in a torrid kiss.

9

Milo leaned against the wall beside Green Pastures' entrance, smoking a cigarette as the AA meeting started to disperse. A ragtag troupe of people exited, going their separate ways, while a few congregated near him, chatting. Marie was one of the last ones out.

"Hi."

She turned, surprised at the sound of his voice. "Oh, Milo. I thought I'd see you inside."

Milo lifted his foot and ground his cigarette against his bootheel, then tossed the butt in a coffee can on the sidewalk.

"Thursdays are hard because the Monsignor has me working at the church till two. This is one of the only meetings I miss during the week."

Marie tentatively smiled, then realized she was standing in the doorway as a couple of stragglers tried to edge past her. Milo took her gently by the arm, and they moved a few paces down the sidewalk.

He smiled at her. "Were you worried about me?"

She blushed. "No, I – just thought you'd be here because of the coffee."

"That's only on Tuesdays. Elmo's got it Wednesday, and Shari's got the coffee commitment today."

They stared at each other for almost a full minute, not saying anything. A couple more people exited the meeting, including a hulking giant of a middle-aged man who looked as if he'd been a linebacker at some point.

"See you tomorrow, Marie." The man shyly waved as he hustled by.

Marie came out of her reverie. "Oh, yeah – see you, Barry."

Milo finally spoke. "What are you doing this afternoon? I have to go meet my friend, Dave, down at the corner cafe in about ten minutes, then I'm free for the rest of the day. Maybe we could catch a movie or get something to eat."

"Well, I – "

"Come on. You're not afraid I'm going to get you into trouble. I know your sober living place has got a not-seeing-guys policy."

"No, it's not that. You've got some time clean, right?"

"Three years."

"We're not going to do anything wrong. I'm not afraid you're going to lead me astray."

Milo smiled, "You never know…"

Marie blushed again and playfully pushed him. "Stop it." She suddenly got more serious. "What they don't know won't hurt them."

She paused, looked away, then back at him.

"It's just – "

"Yeah?

"I'm supposed to go see my little girl at the foster home around 4:30. I don't suppose you would like to come with me?"

It was Milo's turn to be bashful, and he had a doubtful expression as he studied his feet. "I don't know." He glanced back up at her, "I'm not sure if it would be a good idea. I mean, for you. You know, dragging someone like me along."

Marie gave him a sweet smile. "What do you mean, someone like you? Don't be silly. I'd love for you to see her. Would you like to?"

Milo smiled. They started to walk toward the corner. Marie suddenly felt happy. "Then we could go eat and hang out for a little while. Just so I'm back at the place on time. I've got an 8 o'clock curfew for almost another week. Then starting next Tuesday I can stay out till midnight. "

When they reached the intersection. Dave, who was sitting reading a paper at an outside table of the coffee house, looked up at them.

Milo ignored him. "All right. Why don't I meet you back here in about half an hour."

She happily nodded, waved goodbye and, as she looked both ways to cross the street, the green walk signal flashed on. Milo paused for an instant to watch her, taking pleasure in her unassuming grace and sweetness. The sudden honk of a car horn distracted him. Marie slowed to look to her left, and Milo followed her gaze.

It was Carmine's Lincoln with the top down stopping at the red light. But Carmine was MIA, with Rizzo at the wheel and young Anatoli in the passenger seat. The corpulent driver hoisted himself up with difficulty and leaned around the windshield as Marie passed.

"Hey, baby. You're cute."

She quickened her pace, keeping an eye on them, not answering.

Rizzo whined in mock pain, "Hey, don't be like that. We're not gonna hurt you. You're one of those little girls trying to stay off drugs, right?"

Anatoli looked at Milo on the corner, and he tapped Rizzo on the arm. Rizzo was annoyed. "What?"

Anatoli jerked his thumb. "Get a load of the boyfriend."

Marie threw a glance over her shoulder, and Milo nodded to her. She picked up speed, giving the mobsters a cold stare.

Milo waved her on. "Go on, honey. I'll see you in a little while." He smiled as she reached the other side.

Rizzo and Anatoli locked icy eyes with Milo.

"What're you lookin' at, deadbeat?"

The light went green, and a beat-up 1966 Dodge behind the Lincoln honked. Pissed, Rizzo whirled around, kneeling on the seat to glare back at the impatient driver.

"Fuck you!"

Anatoli continued staring at Milo, twisting his neck as Rizzo suddenly peeled angrily off through the intersection.

Dave had remained calmly seated at one of the café's outside tables. He folded his paper and put it down as his friend strolled over and pulled out a chair.

"Those two scumbags. Their boss is who I'm talkin' about rippin' off."

"I know."

A scruffy blond waitress, who seemed as if she might be headed for rehab herself any day, appeared from the shadowy interior and placed one cup of coffee before each of them. Milo took a sip.

Dave leered. "That little chicken your new girlfriend? She *is* cute. Why didn't you introduce me?"

Milo shot Dave a disparaging look as he picked up his coffee.

Milo glanced around the apartment living room. The sun squinting through the puke-brown curtains generated a headachey glare. He settled deeper into the ugly lime-green sofa as Marie nervously fidgeted, perched beside him on the edge of the cushions. He tried to banish his negative thoughts, but the generic image of the pudgy, middle-aged Carla, thoughtfully floating in with glasses of ice tea on a tray, setting it on the spotless discount department-store coffee table, made him think of *The Stepford Wives.*

"So tell me, how's everything going for you?"

"Okay, I guess. I've got a couple lines on a job." Milo could hear the nervousness in Marie's voice and resisted the temptation to reach out to squeeze her hand. "I just miss Rimi, that's what's hardest."

Carla nodded, and there followed an awkward moment of silence. Milo noticed the restless hum and squawk of creeping traffic far down, four floors below.

"I'm sorry, I should go and wake her. She just gets grouchy when she hasn't had her nap. I wouldn't have put her down to sleep if I knew you were coming now. I thought you wouldn't be here for another hour or so, you know, till round the time Phil gets home from work."

A pang of empathy for Marie thumped in Milo's heart as he heard her answer with self-effacing humility. "I'm sorry. This is the time my caseworker told me to come."

Carla put down her tea as she got up. "That's okay. Just give me a minute. I'll be right back."

She disappeared. Marie looked after her, then over at Milo. There was the sound of Rimi crying, and they could make out Carla's muffled voice.

"It's okay, Rimi. Sorry to wake you, sweetie-pie, but your mom stopped by to see you. That's right. Unh-hunh. Come on, honey."

The crying gradually dwindled.

Carla reappeared with a skinny little girl with blonde curls, then placed her in the middle of the floor and sat down again herself. Rimi stared doubtfully at Marie.

Marie was overcome and stretched out her arms. "Hi, honey baby."

Rimi glanced at Carla, not sure what to do, then abruptly, shakily, stood up and stumbled to her foster mother's side. Carla embraced the child.

"It's okay, darling. That's your mom, Marie." She pointed. "And her friend, Milo. They came to visit." She raised her head to look at Marie. "She's a little confused. She hasn't seen enough of you lately." Carla turned Rimi around to face Marie. "Go on, honey. Go over and say hi to your mom."

Rimi peeked up questioningly at Carla, then back at this not quite familiar woman. Suddenly she made tentative steps toward Marie. Rimi fell into her mother's arms, and Marie hoisted her onto her lap. Rimi laughed and smiled back at Carla, then over at Milo. Milo waved at her as Marie hugged her close.

"So did they say anything about when you might get to take her back?"

Yanked from her maternal reverie to icy reality, Marie looked up, uncertain of how honest she should be.

"No, you know…it's too early. I've still got to get a job and a place of my own before that can happen." She hesitated. "I guess they're taking a wait-and-see attitude…to see how I do."

The moment of warmth and calm was shattered as Rimi started crying again. Carla was on her feet without hesitation, plucking Rimi from Marie's grasp. Marie had a deer caught in the headlights expression.

Carla nuzzled the tiny girl. "Oh, yes, yes. You're cranky 'cause we woke you up from your little ole nap... yes, yes, yes." She disappeared from the room with the child in her arms, whisking Rimi back to bed. Milo watched as Marie pivoted anxiously to follow them with moistening eyes.

Milo and Marie sat on a bench, an empty patch of sun-baked, brown grass stretching out behind them in the grungy neighborhood park next to Carla's building. The place didn't feel or look like the surrounding Manhattan, more like they'd been picked up then dropped and stranded somehere in Queens. Marie was bent over, staring into space.

"I'm really frightened, Milo. I'm terrified that by the time I'm together enough to get Rimi back, she's going to have forgotten me. She's not going to know who I am. She'll be too used to Carla and her husband. It's happening already."

"What about your mom? Couldn't she take care of her? Couldn't you go live with your mom when you're done with sober living? And bring Rimi with you?"

Marie sank against the back of the bench, raising and hugging her legs, resting her chin on her knees. "It's impossible. My stepdad's a pig…"

She paused, not wanting to go on. She spat out the next words.

"He's a pig who can't keep his hands to himself. And Mom's got her eyes closed. I don't want to have to paint a detailed picture."

Milo nodded and gazed into the park, studying the rush hour traffic crawling by a half block away. "Hey, why don't you come with me, somewhere nice and quiet, at least compared to this."

Marie glanced at her watch and turned toward him.

Milo grinned. "What time is it? We couldn't have been there for more than 20 minutes."

Marie smiled shyly. "It's almost 5:30."

The late summer sun still hung like a dirty orange lightbulb over the skyline. Milo spread out a clean, flattened patch of cardboard, and the two of them sank against the wall on the shady side of the brick rooftop access. They were on a tenement roof four stories up, and the steeple of St. Margaret's bisected the horizon at the end of the block.

"It's wonderful up here."

Milo laughed. "I wouldn't go that far. But it's a hell of a lot nicer than that shabby excuse for a park. Whenever I can't stand to be around other people, and I want to get away from St. Margaret's, this is where I come."

"Do you live on the church grounds?"

"The basement, yeah. There's a funky little room down there."

Marie leaned over and, as she kissed him on the cheek, something in the sky caught her attention. She pointed. They craned their necks to follow a red balloon floating up into the smog. They were both surprised because there was an abrupt lull in the traffic, and they could hear the breeze in the tree branches on the avenue below. When they looked back at each other, she screwed up her courage and bent over to Milo. She stopped a couple of inches before his face. He stared into her eyes, and the sweetness there drew him closer until his lips brushed hers. He reached up to hold her chin as they kissed.

Milo's and Marie's steps echoed loudly as they walked into the vestibule. He turned off to the left side before they could reach the pews, and Marie followed him as he headed down stone steps leading below.

"It's a good thing the Monsignor's out doing golf and dinner." Milo smiled. "He looks down on me entertaining young ladies in the church." From the absence of Gus and the mobster's black town car out back, Milo was certain Nunzio wasn't around either.

"Wow. I've never been in a church like this before. We were

Catholic but my mom stopped taking me to Mass when I was still in first grade."

Milo glanced at her as he made his way through the cool shadows. They climbed down a few more steps, then entered the long underground passageway. He stopped at the door to his room and unlocked it.

Dusky, dying sunlight filtered in from the tiny window high up on the wall.

"As you can tell, I live the good life."

Milo and Marie sunk down side by side on the narrow cot.

"I like this."

"It's not much."

"I like it. It's a refuge from the city, from the outside world. Almost like being safe back in the womb."

"Yeah? Maybe. But it all depends on whose womb you're in."

They awkwardly sat there for a few minutes, stiff with shyness.

"Milo, I'm so scared."

He put his arm around her, and she nestled into his shoulder. After a few more seconds, she raised her head, and they kissed.

Suddenly, every bit of passion and fear and joy and anger came flooding up out of her. She unbuttoned Milo's shirt, all the while keeping her lips hungrily glued to his, and their kisses evolved into a devouring delirium. She pulled his shirt off, and he helped her lift her dress up over her head. Slowly, as they completely shed their clothes, they stretched out on the narrow cot, caressing and kissing each other.

They lost track of time as they made love. When they finally stopped, Milo noticed the light outside had waned. Time didn't matter. It felt so good just lying there in each other's arms. It was different from the way he felt when he was with Dorrie Reynolds. Not necessarily better, but different. He felt a protectiveness toward this girl. Marie burrowed her head into the crook of his shoulder. She fingered the pendant hanging around his neck.

"What's this?"

"Something from when I was in Nam. It used to belong to my Vietnamese girlfriend." He hesitated. "She got killed in Saigon."

"I'm sorry."

Then she finally noticed the scar on his left shoulder where Jerry had shot him. She gently touched it.

He whispered, "Saigon."

Before he could explain further, the meaning of the twilight struck him, and he grabbed his watch off the floor. "Shit! It's twenty-to-eight. I've got to get you back to your sober living."

Traveling from Manhattan to Marie's Brooklyn halfway house in 20 minutes – there was no way they could make it by her curfew.

10

The sidewalk appeared even dirtier and more squalid in the dusky twilight than it had earlier in the afternoon.

As they walked briskly along, Milo recognized homeless, gimpy Stanley up ahead, loping in the general direction of the Green Pastures storefront. Stanley was around 50, but 30 of them had been spent living hard in the streets and back alleys, and he looked at least ten years older than he was. Suddenly, he paused, undecided, and squinted at the opposite side of the pavement down the block where Sugar, one of Mal's runners, leaned against a lamppost.

Milo tried to divert him. "Hey, Stanley."

Stanley mumbled, "Hey, guys..." but he was too preoccupied with the idea of getting high to turn his head in their direction as they passed.

The sight of such naked craving was like a bucket of ice water on Marie, and she shivered. "Man, he's in another world."

Milo changed the subject, distracted by hunger pangs.

"Damn it. We forgot to get anything to eat before you had to go back."

She smiled but didn't answer, then almost ran into him as he stopped after a couple more paces to turn to watch Stanley. Stanley had begun to cross the street as Sugar moved down the sidewalk to meet him on the other side.

"Hey, Stanley, my man."

Sugar's patronizing tone made Marie want to retch.

When Stanley was almost to the opposite curb, Father Culkin materialized out of the storefront. Milo imagined what was coming and didn't like it.

Then he remembered Marie was on the clock and couldn't afford to tarry. She stole a timid glance at him as he started walking again, and she struggled to keep pace. A few seconds later, they reached the street corner café where she needed to turn and cross.

"You go on ahead, honey. You're gonna be late."

Milo's tone was all brotherly concern, but he wasn't even looking at her, and he absentmindedly stared at the unfolding drama down the block.

"What are you going to do?"

He turned to her and tried to be reassuring, but he realized he was doing a lousy job.

"Nothing. I just want to make sure a hotheaded someone we know doesn't bite off more than he can chew."

His hands planted uneasily in his pockets, he bent over and bussed her on the cheek. "Go on. It'll be okay. Why don't we hook up at tomorrow's meeting."

She nodded. Suddenly, tentatively, she blushingly reached up and kissed him again, but on the lips, then was off across the street. He smiled after her. She swiveled in the crosswalk to wave, but her attention was caught by what was taking place two dozen yards away. She paused at the opposite corner.

Milo pivoted to follow the direction of her gaze.

Father Culkin had hold of Stanley's arm, and the two were waiting for a car to pass to return back to the other side of the street. Sugar reached them just as they pushed off.

Milo waved Marie on. "You're already late, baby. Go on ahead. Everything's okay. Really."

Marie gave him a doubtful frown but nodded and took off along the side street. Milo returned his concentration to Culkin and Stanley.

"Hey, Mister Turned-Around-Collar! Don't be doin' me like that! Where the fuck you taking him?"

Culkin stopped as they stepped up on their side of the curb. He gently but firmly gave Stanley a shove. "Get inside the center, Stanley, and get yourself some coffee."

Stanley craned his neck to stare at Sugar over Culkin's shoulder but did as the priest told him, sulkily shuffling into the storefront.

As Milo got closer, he glimpsed Mal at his apartment window, smoking a cigarette. He had pulled back the curtain, holding it in place with one long-fingered hand, and his callous eyes were studying the situation.

Culkin looked both ways for traffic, then calmly re-crossed the asphalt to confront Sugar. The dealer was clearly getting worked up.

"Don't be playing that holier-than-thou shit with me, sucker!"

Despite the voices inside his brain telling him everything would settle down before coming to a head, Milo was alarmed.

Culkin defiantly put his hands on his hips as he stopped mere inches from Sugar's face. Sugar abruptly leaned over and whispered something in his ear. Culkin erupted, coldcocking Sugar in the face with a balled-up fist, and the man plummeted backwards, landing on the walk with an audible thud, even to Milo halfway down the block. Losing every bit of self-control, the priest jumped on the prone dealer and began to wale.

Milo froze for a few seconds in stupefied shock at Culkin's angry outburst. The rampaging priest reminded him of MP Jerry back in Saigon, and he had a queasy fit of nausea that struck him in the chest. Culkin was running off the rails, going straight off his rocker, grabbing a trash-can lid from a nearby pile of garbage and unrestrainedly bashing it into Sugar's skull.

Something snapped taut inside Milo's head, and he found himself running to the scene. He surveyed the neighborhood as he ran, gauging the expressions of the various tenants perched rapt on their stoops. Some of them looked on in horror. Others laughed, slapping their legs with perverse merriment, and some even shouted out bets on who was going to whup who. Milo was conscious of Mal watching from above as he grabbed Culkin from behind by both arms and yanked him off of Sugar.

"Stop it! You're going to kill him!"

Culkin was still boiling. "I don't want to kill *him!* That no good bastard *up there!*" He pointed above his head at Mal. "That's *who* I want to kill!"

With that, Mal let the curtain fall back into place. It was made out of sheer gossamer material, and Milo could see him through it, stoically igniting another cigarette from the lit butt of the one he was finishing.

Culkin sat on a folding chair with his head in his hands. Stanley still seemed scared, and he cowered next to Milo who was leaning against the table they used at the meetings for the coffee.

"I have to apologize to you, Milo. I don't know -- I don't know what-the-hell I was thinking."

"You weren't thinking."

There was an uncomfortable silence.

"Father, you have to understand people like Sugar and Mal. They're not human. What you just did – I'd be scared if I were you. Being a priest isn't going to help."

"I'm not scared of them."

"Maybe you should be. If it was Carmine and his goombahs, I wouldn't be worried. They're not human either, but they've got all their Catholic upbringing to make them think twice before killing a priest. Not those guys across the street. They don't give a shit."

Culkin rubbed his hands over his face, stood up and walked to the open door. A police car slowly coasted to a halt, double-parking right in front. The two cops looked at each other, then out at Culkin.

"What's shakin', Padre?" asked the one on the passenger side. "We got a call."

"Yeah?"

"Yeah. Someone said there was a ruckus in the neighborhood. You okay?"

"Yeah, sure. I'm fine."

"You wouldn't be kiddin' us now, would you? About being fine?"

"No. Why would I?

"There's a trash can turned over in the driveway across the street and what looks like a patch of blood. Looks pretty fresh. But you wouldn't know anything about that, I take it?"

Culkin hesitated, then finally shook his head.

"Nothing to do with our favorite entrepreneur on the block?" The cop gestured towards Mal's building.

"Nope."

The two cops grinned, glancing at each other. The gabby one shook his head as he looked back at Culkin.

"It's your funeral."

The patrol car rolled down the street. Culkin watched them for a few seconds, then came back in, shutting the door behind him.

"Maybe you shouldn't stay here tonight."

Culkin wouldn't even look at Milo. "I can't *not* be here. People in trouble expect to be able to find me."

"You won't be any good to them if you're dead."

Culkin was getting impatient again. "I'll be okay. Don't worry about my welfare."

Not knowing what else to say, Milo put his hands in his pockets then turned to Stanley.

Stanley shrugged. "Don't look at me."

Milo glanced at Culkin. "I'm going to split, but I'll be back later tonight to check in, make sure everything is all right."

"Suit yourself."

Milo was disgusted with the both of them, but he refrained from saying anything else as he opened the door and left.

Marie was in her room alone, folding laundry. She was grateful her roommate was downstairs, still helping to clean up the kitchen. She brought the pair of jeans up to her nose, inhaling its freshness, trying to distract herself from the smell of vomit in the hall. The little punk teeny bopper next door had been sick that morning, right before she had tested dirty and gotten kicked out. Marie glanced at the shag carpet outside the open door and flinched, feeling nauseous.

Millie, the sober living house manager, appeared and knocked on the doorjamb.

"Can I come in?"

Marie nodded.

"I hate to tell you this, Marie, but I saw you hanging out with that guy, Milo, this afternoon. You know that's against the rules during the first six weeks."

Marie stared dumbly at her but felt as if she'd been punched in the stomach. Crushing the jeans to her breasts with both arms, she slowly sat down on the bed.

"You want me to do a urine test? I didn't do any drugs or drinking. It was… innocent." Then she thought of how good Milo's cock had felt inside of her two hours before and blushed a deep crimson.

Millie sat down on the other end of the bed. "I can tell you didn't get high. That's not the point. I'm not supposed to make exceptions about the not-seeing-guys rule. If I hadn't been with Janet, who's a goddamn big mouth, I could look the other way."

"Millie, you know what it means if I get kicked out of here. I have no place to go. It'll go into my file with my caseworker. Child protective services will hold it against me."

"I don't want to kick you out." She paused and sighed, frowning. "I'm going to have to sleep on it, I guess. I'll let you know tomorrow night."

Millie patted her on the shoulder, got up and walked out. Marie sank back horizontally and gazed at the ceiling. That sucking chest wound was opening up again. She tried to get hold of herself and stave off the anxiety. She visualized herself behind a flimsy door, leaning her whole weight against it while a marauding squad of cruel, faceless monsters tried to break through. Her heart began skipping beats. She knew she was spiraling down and, against every impulse, she forced herself to slowly inhale and exhale deep, even breaths. Gradually, the sensation lessened.

11

Nunzio was in his shirtsleeves in his chair, watching television.

Clad in an oversize flannel shirt, Sara thumped down the stairs and, ignoring her father, quickly crossed the living room into the kitchen.

Big Gus was leaning against the refrigerator, eating a piece of chicken. Sara ignored him, too, and edged him aside as she yanked on the fridge door.

Gus was in good spirits and unfazed by her rudeness. "Hey, Sara, how was the movie last night? What'd you go see?"

She slammed the door, snapped off part of a carrot stick and stuck it in her mouth. She chewed noisily for a few seconds, just looking at him.

"It was an advance screening of this French movie. It's not out yet."

"Oh, yeah, advance screening?" He was oblivious to her condescending tone.

"You know, the distributors were having a screening for publicity, for exhibitors and press. Cecilia had free tickets."

She grabbed a pack of cigarettes and a lighter off the kitchen table.

"Wow. What was it called?"

Bathed in the light from the TV set, Nunzio was eavesdropping and dialed the sound down a bit on the remote to hear better.

"*Le Petit Mort.*"

"La Petty - wha-?"

Sara sighed dramatically. "Haven't you ever heard that expression before? *Le Petit Mort*. It's a metaphor for something else... which I won't go into right now."

Nunzio grimaced. He shook his head with loathing and whispered to himself "Wise ass."

Gus grew more puzzled, "What's a metty-for?"

Sara sighed dramatically, waltzing out of the kitchen followed by the perplexed Gus.

"It means *Little Death*."

On a strange impulse, Sara detoured, bent over and kissed her disgruntled father on the forehead, then continued across the room. He was taken aback.

"Good night, you two."

She waved over her shoulder as she ascended the stairs.

Nunzio and Gus watched her climb the steps.

"She's a funny kid." Gus remained stymied.

"Yeah – " Nunzio returned his attention to the TV as he turned up the volume. " – A real scream."

As soon as Sara had closed the door, she exaggeratedly wiped the back of both her hands across her mouth, trying to erase the contact of the kiss from her lips. She climbed under the bed sheet, lighting a cigarette and picking up a picture from the bedside table in one fluid, angry motion. The photo was a posed head shot of her mother, Andrea, smiling and in her prime, no more than 35 years old. She took a long drag on the cigarette as she studied the image, then with her free hand stubbed it out in an ashtray on the floor. She hugged the framed portrait as she turned on her side and stared into space.

Nunzio had been a little less grey at the temples back then, but otherwise he looked the same. Andrea had just stood there in the kitchen by the back door, coldly watching him. She had had a tumbler full of whiskey in one hand, and the hatred emanating from them both had been like a solid mass.

Nunzio was not happy. He could tell his wife was at the end of her rope, but he didn't care. He was the man, the one who mattered.

"Where are you going every day, Andrea? You're never here!"

"How many times have I told you?"

"School? Are you kidding me? Are you trying to be funny? What would you want with school? Why would someone who has every whim and need taken care of by her husband feel the need to go to school?"

Andrea sneered at his incredulous arrogance and raised the glass to her lips.

"Don't! I told you I didn't want you drinking anymore. You're becoming a goddamn alcoholic. You've got a daughter, too, in case you've forgotten!"

"Fuck you – "

She upended the whiskey into her mouth, gulping it all, while Nunzio looked on, powerless, seething with a growing anger. His veins were sticking out in his forehead. He lashed out, slapping the glass from her hand with one fist and choking her graceful, elegant neck with the other. The glass exploded like a shot on the kitchen floor.

Sara, unable to stand the fighting any longer, ran into the kitchen.

Her father was bending Andrea back over the kitchen table at a crazy angle, strangling her. She gasped for air, clawing and kicking at him.

"Daddy! Stop it! Goddamn it, Daddy!"

She tried to pull him off, but he roughly put one hand in her face and pushed her to the floor. She landed on the broken glass.

"Stay out of this!" He sounded completely deranged. "Get upstairs!"

He didn't notice, even as Sara awkwardly picked herself up, that her legs were bleeding.

Out of nowhere, Andrea managed to land a punch in one of his eyes and, in reflex, Nunzio ricocheted off of his wife, banging into the refrigerator and holding his face. Andrea grabbed her purse and the pint of whiskey from the side counter, then scurried out the back door.

Sobbing uncontrollably, Sara clumsily ran out after her.

Andrea fumbled in her bag for her keys as she bumped into the car, frantically unlocking it, continually glancing over her shoulder to see if Nunzio was behind her. Sara stopped a few feet away, but Andrea stared right through her as if she wasn't there.

"Mama, don't! Please don't!"

She tried to latch onto her mother as she jumped into the car, but Andrea shoved her away. Sara slipped and fell onto the asphalt driveway. Her weeping began to come in big, hiccoughing gasps. Andrea switched on the ignition, revved the gas, threw the gear into reverse and craned her neck around to back up.

At last, she noticed Sara and paused, slamming on the brakes, the idling engine softly roaring. They locked eyes for only a few seconds.

Tears streamed down Andrea's cheeks, but her sobbing wasn't audible. She smiled a sad smile.

"Goodbye, baby...I'm so, so sorry."

Andrea let her foot off the brake, stomped on the gas and rocketed backwards out of the driveway just as a huge panel truck was speeding down the street. The truck plowed right into her with a deafening crash, ramming the car down the block and out of sight.

Sara stood up, but she felt as if she was slipping into shock.

"Mama, oh, Mama. No, Mama. No, no, no."

Sara wiped away a tear, pulled up her sheet, then reached over and turned off her bedside lamp.

Marie was propped up on two pillows, reading by the light in between the twin beds. Her roommate, Janet, tossed and turned across from her. Finally, she sprang up on one arm.

"I wouldn't want to impose, but could you please...*turn out the fucking light!*"

Marie didn't look at her as she slowly closed the book and put it down. She reached over to the lamp and switched it off. She lay there in the dim room, staring at the ceiling. She still wasn't used to turning in so early. To make matters worse, the room was sweltering. It was too hot to sleep.

12

The karate school was about a 15-minute walk into a more stable neighborhood than Green Pastures, closer to Park Slope, and was dotted with yellow pools of light spilling from storefronts and restaurants.

Milo hurried down the busy sidewalk, preoccupied with a feeling of impending doom that he could not shake. When he reached the school, he paused at the enormous window that took up most of the front of the building. A group of about 17 students were practicing in the middle of the huge chamber. Three were already done and going into the changing room to get into their street clothes. One of them was Jack. He caught sight of Milo as he was coming through the front door.

"Hey, man." He happily shouted across the high-ceilinged space. "What're you doing here?"

Milo shrugged and sat down on one of the chairs near the entrance as Jack walked up to him.

"Give me a minute. I've just got to get dressed." Wiping his face and neck with a towel, Jack slipped into the locker room. Milo watched the other students while he waited. A siren welled up, then wailed by outside. Milo glanced nervously out the window, staring after the flashing red light as it disappeared down the block.

"Hey, what's up?"

Milo turned to face Jack, who was already dressed and finishing buttoning his shirt. "That was fast."

"I didn't shower. What's the use? It's so hot and humid I'd have to take another one by the time I got home. I was going to try to get in touch with you as soon as I left to see if you wanted to get a bite to eat."

"Yeah? What's going on with Anne?"

"She's over at her folks. Won't be back till around midnight."

Milo said nothing and glanced again into the street.

"What's up with you? You're acting weird."

"Some shit went down outside Culkin's drug and alcohol center this afternoon."

"Yeah? Involving you?"

"In a way – " Milo stood up. "You ready to leave? Let's walk."

Jack was right. It was hot and humid and not cooling off at all, despite the sun having just gone down. In fact, it seemed to be getting worse.

Milo told him what happened.

"Shit. Culkin kicked his butt? One of Mal Powers' dealers?"

Milo nodded.

"I never would have thought he had it in him."

"It was a really stupid thing for him to do. He knows better. He's always had that hot temper. Why do you think he's not at St. Margaret's anymore? Monsignor Al had enough of his back talk and kicked him out on his ass. He's lucky he hasn't been defrocked yet."

They paused outside a pizza place, and Jack looked in the window.

"I'm sorry, I've got to eat. I haven't had anything since noon."

"Me, too."

Milo and Jack each picked up a couple of slices at the counter, paid, then settled at a table. Milo drank water while Jack nursed a beer.

"I'm not sure what to do. I have a bad feeling...like something's going to happen later."

Jack smiled. "You want me to come down and camp out with you and Culkin and whoever the resident homeless junkie is?"

Milo laughed.

"Well, that's about it, am I right?"

"I don't know. What do you think?"

Jack chugged the rest of his beer in answer. They both had already wolfed down their pizza. Jack stood up, energized, wiped his mouth and patted his chest theatrically.

"Let's go."

They walked back into the night.

"You get your manuscript turned in?"

"Yeah. All done, at long last."

For a minute or so, they walked quickly in silence.

"So why didn't you get in touch with Dave? He beats me hands- down in the badass department."

"He'd give me shit about it. Then, if anything did happen, he'd go way over the top. Someone would get wasted."

Jack smiled. "And we wouldn't want any drug dealers to get wasted."

Milo laughed. "Not at Culkin's, anyway."

The heat dissipated only slightly as they made their way further east. The walk seemed interminable, and they didn't talk much after the first few minutes.

Finally Green Pastures was in front of them. The lights in the big main meeting room were still on though it looked empty, and Milo peeked in the front window before they entered. They plunged into shadow for a few seconds as they passed behind the partition that jutted from the inside of the door. The overhead fluorescent lights created an eerie glow in the cold looking chamber. All the chairs for the meetings were stacked up against the far wall.

Stanley lay on a cot against the opposite corner by the kitchen entrance, his backside to them. His snores were deafening. The pair approached, Milo turning to Jack with a quieting finger to his lips. Their shadows loomed on the wall. Suddenly, Stanley became aware of their presence and practically somersaulted around in panic, landing on his ass on the floor.

"What's going on there, Stanley? Think Sugar was sneaking up on you?"

Stanley refused to look at Milo as he picked himself up and shuffled hurriedly to the coffeemaker on the counter. He glanced over his shoulder as he poured himself a cup.

"You guys are assholes."

"Sorry, Stanley. Maybe you should've locked the front door."

Stanley sipped the bitter, scalding liquid.

"Father Culkin likes to keep it open till ten in case somebody needs to come in to talk. Shit, Milo, you're the AA poster boy around here. Don't you know his MO by now?"

Milo decanted some coffee, offered it to Jack who demurred, then took a sip of it himself.

"I think he could have made an exception after the little

wrestling match he and Sugar got into this afternoon. He's liable to have some visitors."

"Nobody asked your opinion, Milo."

The three turned as Culkin walked down the last few steps of the stairs in the darkened kitchen and then into the main meeting room.

"I don't need your help. And I'm not going to start running scared 'cause I had a little set-to with that shit-for-brains scumbag from across the street."

Milo and Jack looked at each other, then back at Culkin. Milo felt indignant. "I don't mean to be condescending, but you need some other people around you right now."

Culkin gestured at Jack. "Who's this?"

"Jack Arabella. A friend. You've met before, though it's been a while. He's got a brown belt in karate."

Culkin fought a smile as he softened. "Listen, you guys, I don't need your help. I appreciate the thought, but I can take care of myself."

"Well, let me finish my coffee, at least."

Culkin grimaced, nodded, then checked his watch. "Maybe it wouldn't be such a bad idea to lock the door. It's almost ten now anyway."

The three watched him as he walked across the room and disappeared behind the fake wood partition. Milo shook his head.

Stanley whispered. "Boy, he sure is somethin' else."

All three stiffened as they saw Culkin reappear. Rizzo, Anatoli, Gino, Sugar and Mal Powers steered the priest into the room in front of them at the point of a gun. Sugar's left arm and forehead were bandaged. Massive purple bruises reflected on his dark swollen face. Rizzo gestured with his gun to Gino, who promptly strode to the giant window and lowered the two sets of venetian blinds.

Rizzo was extremely amused. "Well, will you look at this, Mal. We got a mini-teetotaler convention going on here."

Mal grinned. "Sure do. And some of my favorite people. Mr. Stanley, the high-rollin' hipster – Stanley, he my man! Mister Holier-Than-Thou Milo who always is so damn polite – used to be one of my best customers back in the day – and he never fails to say 'hey' when he sees me. And last but not least Mister Jack, The Towering Sensitive Intellect – " he turned slightly toward Sugar, "I bet you didn't know that Jack here is married to a sister."

Sugar sniggered. "Yeah? She a white-looking bitch?"

Jack was starting to do a slow burn.

Rizzo laughed. "No shit! Jack here is married to a lady of

color? What-do-you-know, we got our own little rainbow coalition right here on the avenue." Rizzo rolled his eyes at Gino and Anatoli, trying to keep a straight face. "Kinda warms your heart, don't it."

Mal suddenly yanked Culkin by the scruff of the neck and tripped him so he went sprawling on the linoleum.

Stanley was shaking like a leaf, with Milo and Jack standing stock still in front of him. Culkin dusted himself off and slowly moved to stand. Mal and Rizzo took a few steps in front of their thug partners. Rizzo waved his gun at the priest.

"No, no, no, Father, stay put. Mal got you down on the ground for a reason."

"That's right. We wanted you to have to look up at us."

"In fact, you three – all yous!" Rizzo waved the gun up and down at Milo, Jack and Stanley. "On the floor – now!"

The three reluctantly joined Culkin sitting cross-legged. The other hoods remained stationary, but Rizzo and Mal began to circle around the seated quartet from opposite directions.

Rizzo nodded at Mal. "Go ahead. Speak your piece."

"I saw what happened this afternoon, *Reverend*." He sarcastically drawled. "Right on my front steps. As much as I'd sometimes love to, I don't come over and wale the tar out of you and yours on the sidewalk outside your door, *now do I*? No, no, I don't. But you -- there was some kind of strange, weird calculatin' goin' on inside that do-gooder brain of yours this afternoon, fomentin' and bubblin' till it broke the surface and exploded. And my man, Sugar, had to take the brunt of your bullshit."

Rizzo chimed in. "He's right, Father. I usually don't step in on stuff like this. But I wanted to make an example. You're upsetting the – what you call it? – *equilibrium*? Yeah, the equilibrium of the whole neighborhood."

Culkin chuckled to himself, and it slowly, steadily built into uproarious laughter. Rizzo, Mal and their men, plus the seated three on the floor, were all startled by Culkin's reaction.

Mal abruptly kicked Culkin hard in the face. Jack immediately jumped up. Milo tried to restrain him, but Rizzo had already leaned forward to bash his gun into the side of Jack's head. Jack slumped down beside the now prone Culkin, groaning and holding his left ear.

"Not smart. Not smart at all."

"My distinguished friend, Mr. Rizzo, came along for another reason, too."

"Let me tell it, Mal." The portly mafioso squatted in front of the on-the-floor men. "I thought it might be a good opportunity to do a little research. A little detective work." He glanced up at Gino for a second. "Hey, Gino, did you know that my cousin used to be a private detective?"

"Yeah?"

"Yeah. Right up until the time he started workin' for the Feds. After that, it was kind of hard to get information out of him, what with his concrete galoshes weighing him down in the East River." He snorted a laugh. "Anyway…I digress."

Rizzo took out his car keys with his free hand and tossed them to Anatoli. "Go get me the bicycle chain."

Anatoli smiled, nodded and quickly disappeared.

Rizzo rested his gaze on Milo. "Gentlemen -- especially you, Milo -- I figure you all might be able to provide some information about who is going 'round rippin' off and whackin' the dealers in Manhattan, the Bronx and here in our very own Brooklyn. You know, *these last few weeks.* Word is it's a white man."

Stanley piped up. "Hey, man, you know me, I don't have nothin' to do with anything around here or anything these guys do. So, can you let me go?"

Rizzo was annoyed. "Your bad luck to be here when we showed up, wino. You should've been in your cardboard box in some alley coppin' 'z's by now. To be blunt, no…no, you can't fuckin' go. Nobody's leaving here till I'm done. So shut your fuckin' pie-hole before I shut it for yous."

Dave had just left the café down the street and was walking. He was going nowhere in particular, and he was thinking of heading home when he saw something up ahead that had made him duck into a doorway. The guinea kid, Anatoli, was skulking out of Green Pastures, nervously looking about and then unlocking the door to the black Cadillac at the curb.

Another four or five doors down the block in the opposite direction, a smartly dressed Asian man came out of a liquor store. It was Yuen, but Dave hadn't seen him in years, didn't recognize him and paid him no mind.

Yuen stopped as he saw what was going on in front of the storefront rehab.

Dave materialized behind Anatoli as the kid got the car door open, banging him over the head with the butt of his silenced automatic and shoving him prone onto the front seat.

He rummaged through Anatoli's pockets and pulled out a .38, pocketed it, then yanked the groggy Anatoli up out of the car, pushing him through the rehab entrance.

Yuen recognized Dave right away. He couldn't believe his luck.

Inside Green Pastures, Anatoli slowly, stiffly appeared around the partition jutting out from the entrance.

"About fucking time. What you doin' out there? Jackin' off?" Rizzo noticed the kid was empty-handed. "Fuck! Can't you do anything right? Where's the – " He stopped mid-sentence as Anatoli moved further into the room. Dave materialized behind him with the gun barrel pointed behind the kid's right ear.

"Shit, who the fuck are you?" Rizzo was supremely annoyed.

"Drop the gun, you fat fuck."

In answer, Rizzo cocked his piece and put it to Culkin's head. Culkin went rigid.

"You're bluffin', motherfucker. You daffy shit. You drop the gun. I'll blow this goddamn priest away!"

Dave was in a cold-blooded mood. "Go ahead. I could give a shit."

Jack yelled, "Dave!" and Milo grabbed Jack's arm to shut him up.

"Go ahead and blow him away. What are you waiting for, you guinea bastard? I'd love it. It'll give me an excuse to execute every one of you."

There were rivers of sweat pouring down Anatoli's blood-streaked face. Everyone was dead quiet. Rizzo was starting to falter. Nerves were shredding inside every one of them, except Dave.

Sugar suddenly freaked as he was struck by a startling revelation. "Oh, fuck, Mal. Now I know him. I've seen him around our places down on Atlantic and across the river on Avenue A. He's gotta be the one! He's gotta be the maniac who's heisting everybody!"

Dave aimed, pulled the trigger and his gun went *pffft!* Sugar crashed to the floor with a bullet through his eye. Dave then kicked Anatoli in the ass towards Rizzo, who reflexively shoved him aside. Anatoli landed prone on the floor, shaking, his hands covering his head in terror.

A cacophony of gunfire erupted from Rizzo and Mal, punctuated by sporadic *phht-phht!* noises from Dave's silenced automatic.

Jack did a spinning kick to Rizzo's ample stomach, toppling

him into Mal, and both thugs tumbled to the floor.

Stanley, Jack and Milo pulled Culkin to the serving bar partition that divided the big room from the kitchen. Stanley slithered over the counter like a nocturnal insect and was gone through the kitchen's rear door in a flash, gliding out of sight into the alley.

Slow-witted Gino fumbled with his gun, trying to get the safety off. Rizzo and Mal overturned a table against the far wall, using it as cover and, in the process, knocked most of the stacked chairs over, which noisily clattered amidst the gun blasts.

Dave gracefully, calmly shifted in front of Milo and Jack, shielding them as he calmly poured muffled lead at the hoods, killing Gino in the process. Out of bullets, Dave nonchalantly dropped out the clip and replaced it.

Suddenly, there was another silenced automatic's *phht-phht!* that barely missed Dave, causing him to cringe and turn.

Hot lead riddled the coffee maker. Scalding brown liquid spurted onto Culkin, and he reflexively moved away from Milo and Jack, who were trying to yank him over the counter into the kitchen.

Yuen peeked from behind the partition and squeezed off two more muffled shots.

Dave crouched, quietly firing. Another burst came from Yuen's weapon, and Culkin, who had moved to shield Milo and Jack, got one in the brain and crumpled. Yuen reloaded.

Milo and Jack were stunned at Culkin's sudden death.

Dave leapt backward over the counter just as Yuen started a new barrage, and Rizzo and Mal opened up again. He landed beside the crouching Milo and Jack.

Milo nudged Dave. "Who the fuck is that other guy?"

Reaching over the counter to let off a couple of shots, Dave answered, "Not one of their regulars. Some gook with an eyepatch." Dave glanced at Milo. "The priest dead?"

Milo nodded.

Dave grimaced. "Shit. He was a crazy motherfucker."

Jack was disgusted. "Look who's talking."

Dave got angry. "You two get the fuck outta here, now."

"We can't leave you here."

"Don't give me that horseshit, Milo. You know me better than that. I'm gonna give it another couple a minutes till you guys have a good lead, then I'm outta here, too. Get the fuck going!" Suddenly, he stood up, calmly firing at Rizzo, Mal and Yuen.

Milo latched onto Jack, and they dove through the rear door

into the alley.

They were in Jack and Anne's kitchen in the narrow Park Slope house. Milo dabbed disinfectant onto Jack's wound on the left side of his forehead and on his ear. Jack winced.

"I guess you saw a lot of that kind of thing in Nam."

Milo was distracted. "What?"

"Ow!"

"Hold still..."

"You know, people getting their brains blown out."

Milo put down the cotton and let out a deep breath. "Not as much as you'd think." He handed Jack a gauze pad. "Press that against it."

Jack took it and held it to the ugly abrasions.

"I was in Saigon at least half of the time. I sometimes saw stuff running interference for Dave."

Jack didn't say anything for a few seconds. "Ever kill anyone?"

Milo was caught off guard. He hesitated and looked down at the linoleum floor. "A couple of times."

There was the sound of the front door being unlocked and someone coming in the living room.

"Anyone home?" It was Anne.

Milo called out. "In here..."

Anne rounded the corner from the dimly lit living room. She stopped short when she saw them. She rushed up to Jack.

"What the hell happened?"

She took hold of Jack's face, gently peeled away the cotton and studied the wounds. She petulantly looked from one to the other. "Well? Somebody gonna tell me?"

Jack turned sheepish, "We got jumped..."

"Unh, hunh. And?"

"We went to a movie in Times Square -- "

Milo chimed in. "We were up in the balcony and told the wrong people to shut the fuck up..."

Anne just stared at them, unsure whether they were telling the truth or not. Annoyed, she snatched the roll of bandages from Milo.

"I'll do it."

Jack held the gauze and cotton pad in place as she wound the bandage around his head.

"I swear, you two. I've about had it. You're just like a couple of kids. And you're both over 40."

Milo and Jack glanced at each other. Anne finished, and Milo handed her the metal butterfly catch to hold the dressing in place. Depressed, Jack tenderly kissed Anne on the cheek and walked slowly into the living room.

Milo and Anne locked stares, saying nothing. Finally, Anne looked away.

There was the sound of Jack turning on the TV. He switched channels, and a news broadcast blared. There was the trebly squawk of an announcer's voice: *" – news team. We'll talk about your money and weather in just a moment, but first this late-breaking story about a triple murder, what appears to be a gangland-style massacre at a Brooklyn storefront church that also doubles as a kind of rehab clubhouse center for recovering drug addicts and alcoholics..."*

Milo left Anne standing there alone. She was disgusted and had an unpleasant intuition gnawing at her guts that she tried to keep at bay. She joined Milo in the kitchen doorway.

Jack was lying on the couch, and the TV cast a ghostly, cold blue light from the other side of the room. The announcer's voice continued: *"...three men were killed by multiple gunshots in what appeared to be a frantic gun battle. Police were drawn to the scene by the sound of the shots..."*

Anne looked sideways at Milo, then back at the TV.

"Only one of the dead men has so far been identified, a priest named Father James Culkin, who lived at the center and acted as pastor for the homeless and recovering addicts who were his congregation. At this time, the other two persons have, as yet, not been identified – one a Caucasian male about 40 who may be of Italian-American descent, the other, an African-American male about 30. We'll keep you posted as we receive updates on this late-breaking story..."

A commercial for dog food was suddenly blasting twice as loud as the news. Anne walked to the cluttered glass coffee table, picked up the remote and switched off the TV. She glanced down at Jack, stretched out on the sofa and now asleep. Milo watched from the lighted doorway as she pulled a blanket from the top of the couch and tenderly placed it over her husband. She walked past Milo into the kitchen. He joined her and wearily slumped up against the back door. Anne opened a beer, leaning against the sink. She gestured towards the TV in the living room.

"Did you know about that already? You don't seem too surprised. That's the place where you sometimes go to AA meetings, right? You knew that priest. I met him myself that time when Jack and I came to your two-year sober anniversary -- "

Milo couldn't meet her eyes and peered at the floor.

"I have a bad feeling, Milo. You don't want to even know what I'm thinking..."

"What? That we were there?"

"I don't know and, frankly, I don't want to know. But I do know one thing, I want you to stop hanging out with Jack for a while."

"Anne...I... "

"You can't even think of anything to say, can you?" Anne lowered her voice and moved closer to him. "You know I'm right. It's been like this ever since high school, Milo. Jack's always looked up to you. You were the guy that went out and did things, lived a crazy, adventurous life while Jack, 'cause he took school seriously, just sat around and dreamed about it. When you two graduated, you got forced into the Army, and he felt guilty. He got his student deferment for college – "

In the living room, their voices had disturbed Jack's fragile sleep. He restlessly turned on his side, facing the couch cushions, but his eyes were open, and he was listening.

"–I know he didn't really want to go to Vietnam, he didn't believe in it. But he would have gone, had cooler heads around him – like me and his mother – not prevailed. He missed you. We both missed you. And he felt guilty because he didn't go. And he didn't know if he'd ever see you again. Why do you think he took up the karate?"

Milo didn't say anything as she paused, but he raised his head to look at her.

"Trying to prove something to himself," she continued, whispering. "That he was a man, too, while he still read his books and did his writing and sat at home and dreamed. Some might think it's stupid or foolish, but it made me love him as much as I ever loved you -- "

She paused again, her eyes growing wet. "Ultimately, it made me love him even more..."

They both were quiet, staring at each other. Milo reached out and caressed her cheek.

There was the sound of a metallic click and a soft tread stopping in the kitchen doorway.

Yuen calmly stood there, holding his silenced automatic on them. He smiled. Milo pushed Anne away as he smashed himself against the refrigerator. There was a *phht-phht!* as the gun went off twice, and a bullet hit Milo just above his left wrist.

Jack appeared, tackling Yuen, crashing him sideways into a cabinet, breaking a small Virgin Mary statue and toppling a stand-up lamp. He slammed Yuen's gun arm, and it went off again, shattering the TV screen in a loud pop of smoke, sparks and broken glass. The two men frantically clutched at each other, overturning furniture.

Milo, pressing a dish towel to his bleeding forearm, joined Anne in the doorway, and edged in front of her to shield her.

Jack karate chopped Yuen's arm, causing him to drop the automatic, and it skittered across the hardwood floor to the far side of the room.

Without warning, Yuen shifted under Jack, heaved upwards and flipped him so he landed on top of the glass coffee table, shattering it.

Anne screamed, "Goddamn it, why are you doing this! What-the-fuck do you want here!" She tried to get around Milo, and he ran interference, with limited success, to hold her back.

Jack rolled away just as Yuen leapt up and down, aiming for his chest. In one fluid motion, Jack picked up the end of the toppled upright lamp, swinging it into Yuen's side, causing him to lose his footing and go down. Jack jumped, kicking Yuen in the head. Stunned, but not seriously hurt, he quickly regained his feet. Both of the men were bleeding from cuts on their faces and hands. They warily circled each other.

Anne moaned. "Please, stop it! Jack, please – "

Milo tried to edge into the room past the two fighting men, sliding sideways toward the distant gun, but Yuen lashed out. Milo flung himself backwards so he wouldn't catch the full brunt of Yuen's blow and landed on the couch. Jack took the opportunity to grab Yuen's arms from behind, but Yuen crashed backwards, sending Jack into a bookcase which tottered, showering paperbacks and hardbound books all around them.

Yuen repeatedly jabbed at Jack's throat, but Jack warded off the blows with his arms. He advanced, but Yuen faked a lunge backwards, then sidestepped, moving to his right, tripping Jack and throwing him sideways to the floor. Jack landed on upraised shards of the glass coffee table, and one of them pierced his neck, slicing his jugular.

Anne screamed.

Yuen stood there, weaving uncertainly, dazed as he looked down at Jack.

Milo lunged for the gun on the floor, secured it and pointed it at Yuen.

Yuen deftly circled around Jack's convulsing body, keeping his eye on Milo as he tried to make for the open front door.

Oblivious now to the still deadly contest of wills between Yuen and Milo, Anne dropped down to her knees at Jack's side, holding him in her arms as he tried to reach out to her, tried to say her name but could not speak. The spurting blood drenched everything, and she hysterically tried, without success, to staunch the flow.

Surprisingly, Yuen seemed disturbed that he had fatally wounded Jack. But he was too much of a pro to let it throw him and distract him from Milo. He dove through the open door as Milo squeezed off a silent shot. The bullet splintered the doorjamb, missing its target. Milo leapt to his feet and ran out of the house.

Jack kept trying to speak, but his efforts diminished as the light quickly waned in his eyes, and then his lids closed halfway. Suddenly he was dead. Beside herself, Anne was so traumatized her weeping came in nearly soundless gasps; her caressing and obsessive holding of Jack, gentle but spastic.

Outside, the block was quiet.

Milo stood in the middle of the street, staring after Yuen, who had disappeared into the darkness. Holding the gun at his side, Milo turned and walked across the microscopically poor excuse for a front yard, climbing the steps to the house.

Anne clutched Jack to her bosom and looked up angrily when she heard Milo.

He stopped in the doorway and stared dumbly at his dead friend. Furious with grief, she mercilessly castigated him.

"God-fucking-damn-you, Milo! God-fucking-damn-you! Who was that? He wasn't here for Jack, he was here for you! He knew you!"

Milo couldn't speak. His voice was gone, his throat dry and constricted.

"And *you knew* him!" she shouted.

Milo could no longer meet her gaze.

"How dare you get Jack involved in your fucked-up shit!"

Milo took a step toward her.

"No, stay the fuck away from us. All you've ever brought the two of us is misery. You're a goddamn jinx. A goddamn-walking-and-talking-piece-of-bad-luck. Get out!"

He slowly turned, numb and grief-stricken himself. He stumbled through the front door. He realized he still held the gun tightly in his right hand, and he tucked it inside his denim jacket. Blood dripped from his wounded left forearm as he stiffly made his way down the porch steps. He could still hear Anne's gentle sobbing.

Neighbors from both sides, their voices discreet murmurs, had appeared on their puny, adjoining lawns, curiously staring after Milo. Then, once he'd passed them, they tentatively climbed onto the porch and went into Anne and Jack's house.

Milo strode down the middle of the street.

13

Nunzio, clad in slacks and a partially unbuttoned white shirt, sat at his kitchen table, angry as hell and nervously chewing his fingernails. He had a newspaper spread out before him.

Gus hung up the wall phone next to the refrigerator and poured himself a cup of coffee.

"Well? Where the fuck is he?"

Gus shyly looked at his boss and tried to adopt a placatory tone. "He left 20 minutes ago. He should be here any second." He softened his voice even more. "Try to calm down, boss."

Nunzio gave him a dirty look. "Don't fuckin' tell me to calm down." He smacked the newspaper. "Look at this shit!" He abruptly wadded it into a ball and threw it at Gus.

There was a knock on the kitchen door. Gus opened it, and Carmine, already dressed to the nines, entered, breathless.

"Sorry I didn't get here sooner. The traffic was nuts. You know, your driveway's blocked. I finally had to park three blocks away and walk. Damn Rizzo. I don't know where the hell he was this morning. If I'd've found him, he could've dropped me off."

Nunzio was doing a slow burn. "You've always got an excuse for everything, don't you? What about last night? What was the excuse for that?"

Carmine stiffened. Alarm bells were finally starting to go off.

"What about last night...what happened?"

Carmine looked questioningly from Nunzio to Gus. He

seemingly hadn't heard about the bloody fiasco. Nunzio pointed at the balled-up newspaper on the floor.

"Pick it up, dunsky."

Carmine was still slow on the uptake. "What?"

"The newspaper, you clueless fuck!"

Carmine retrieved it, carefully unfolding the wad of fragile paper and then studying the front page. At first, his face darkened, then the blood drained from his complexion. He turned, stricken, and stupidly stared at his boss.

Nunzio suddenly lunged from his chair, took Carmine by one lapel and slapped him back-and-forth across the face. Then he banged him against the refrigerator so violently, Carmine slipped and fell on his ass.

Sara heard the commotion and appeared in the doorway.

Nunzio dragged Carmine back up and pinioned him against the refrigerator door by his throat.

"Daddy, stop!" Sara tried to pull her father off, but Nunzio lashed out, roughly pushing her with his left hand so she struck the opposite wall. Gus went to stand by her, and he put a beefy paw on one of her arms.

Nunzio pointed at her with his left hand while holding Carmine up. "Stay out of this, you." He returned his attention to Carmine. "Now correct me if I'm – " he banged Carmine's head against the top freezer door to emphasize the word, "– wrong, but Gino Moscalone was one of the main boys in your crew, right?"

Nunzio bounced Carmine's head against the refrigerator again. "Right?"

Carmine was beyond rattled. "Yeah...right."

"So maybe you wouldn't mind tellin' me what he was doin' getting himself whacked in the company of that crazy priest and that nigger pusher?"

"I don't know. I didn't know about it till just now when you showed me the newspaper. I swear to God!"

Nunzio relaxed his grip a little. "That piece-of-shit storefront, that clubhouse for brain-scrambled dope fiends and skid-row drunks, where this little garden party happened, it's right across the street from where your *moolignon* buddy, Mal Powers, lives. Am I right?"

Carmine nodded. Nunzio released him, sighed deeply, smoothed back his oily disheveled hair with both hands, then suddenly realized his daughter was standing there with Gus. He gestured toward her as he calmed down.

"Sara, go on upstairs. I forgot you were down here. You shouldn't be listening to this."

She stared at him with eyes full of poison.

Nunzio colored under her defiant gaze. "Go on, you heard me. I don't want to go losing my temper at you. You can come back down in a few minutes and have your breakfast."

She stormed off, and the shamed Carmine tried not to look after her.

Nunzio gestured to him.

"Sit down."

Carmine hesitated.

"Go ahead. Sit down. What-the-fuck're you waitin' for!"

Nunzio poured two cups of coffee, then placed one in front of Carmine and one at his own place.

"I don't have to tell you what I want you to do, now do I, Carmine? You know."

Carmine nodded.

"I think you know what I want you to do, but I want you to tell me, just so I'm sure."

Carmine tried to steady his voice, but the words still came out nervous. "You – you want me to find out what happened – why one of my crew, one of your men got himself killed over there."

Nunzio barely smiled as he took a sip from the steaming cup.

"Drink your coffee."

Marie walked briskly in the direction of Green Pastures but slowed when she saw people milling around out front. There was police crime tape stretched across the entrance, and one uniformed cop stood guard. One of the people, a slacker named Tony, turned to face her as she approached.

"Hey, Marie. You hear what went down? Culkin and a couple other guys got murdered last night."

The color went out of Marie's face. She stammered. "Do...do they know who the other guys were?"

He shrugged, unfazed. "One was that drug dealer who always hangs out down on the corner, you know, Sugar."

"How about the other guy?"

"Hey, you know I heard Culkin got in a really hairy brawl with Sugar yesterday afternoon. Probably what started this whole damn thing. Can you believe that? Goddamn priest getting in a fist fight with a drug dealer? You can't make this shit up." Tony thought it was hilarious, even though the priest who'd led many a meeting and had helped him stay sober was lying naked on a slab in the morgue.

Marie repeated her question, growing impatient. "Who was the other guy that got killed?"

"Some white dude, I can't remember his name."

Marie twisted around toward the street, feeling sick.

"Hey, don't get so freaked out. It wasn't anybody from here at the meetings. It was some mob guy, I think."

She slowly faced him.

"Think I heard the name Gino."

"You seen Milo?"

"Nah." Abruptly something occurred to Tony, and he got excited. "Hey, you know who's in town? That guy you used to go out with, the keyboard player from Todos Santos, Stefan."

Marie was distracted. "Yeah?"

"Yeah, he told me to tell you that he'd love to see you if I ran into you. He's staying at the Chelsea in Manhattan. I was going to go over and see him now, since there's no meeting. You want to come?

"I don't know. I should try to find Milo."

"You can do that later. C'mon, it'll be fun."

"He still getting high?"

Tony frowned, looking at his feet. He kicked at a bloodstain on the sidewalk. "Don't know, didn't ask."

Seeing the dried blood on the walk made up Marie's mind. "I'm going to see if I can find Milo, see if he knows about this."

She could tell Tony's feelings were hurt, but she didn't care. He tried to act indifferent. "Okay, whatever. Hey, I'll give you Stefan's cell number..." He scrawled it on a slip of paper. "...give us a call after you're done, see if we're still there."

Marie took the number. "Sure."

Marie didn't see anyone when she entered the shadowy coolness inside St. Margaret's. She peered into the darkness as she headed downstairs, hoping she was remembering the right way. At last, she arrived in the cellar, and she tentatively walked down the dim corridor to Milo's room. She stopped at his door, jumpy as hell for some reason that she could not fathom, and she looked both ways down the stone hall before knocking.

There was no answer.

She knocked again, speaking in a low voice.

"Milo? Milo…are you there?"

She waited a full minute, then decided to leave.

The 1975 Cougar was parked across the street from Anne's parents' house in Prospect Heights.

Stoic Dave sat in the driver's seat. A grief-stricken Milo, clad in a plain black suit coat, a buttoned white shirt that revealed a T-shirt underneath and blue jeans, was hunched against the opposite door. His left forearm was bandaged, including the palm of his hand, the white swath of dressing disappearing beneath his shirt cuffs. He threw an almost-done smoke out the window.

"I'm telling you, man, this is a stupid idea."

Milo shot him a withering look, then opened his door and climbed out.

Dave muttered to himself, hitting the steering wheel in rhythm. "Stupid…stupid, stupid, stupid." He leaned out the window to call after Milo as he started to cross the street. "I'll be waiting for you. You won't be long."

Milo walked the path lined with withered rosebushes, then stepped onto the porch. An ancient brown-skinned man with snow-white hair, dressed in a brown three-piece suit, sat on a stool at the opposite end, smoking a cigar. He looked like one of Anne's uncles, and he pointedly ignored Milo. Milo took a deep breath, looked back at Dave's car across the street and knocked on the door.

There was the sound of footsteps approaching. The door opened to reveal a slightly heavy, though still handsome, black woman in her sixties. It was Anne's mother, Sheila.

"I'm sorry, Milo. She doesn't want to see you."

Milo began to say something but couldn't get the words out. Suddenly Anne's father was towering over Sheila's shoulder.

"What the fuck do *you* want? You're not welcome here. Get your goddamn candy ass off my property."

Sheila whirled on her husband, appalled at his language. "Wendell! I can handle this. Don't make things worse than they are already."

Daggers flashed from Wendell's eyes as he turned, muttering, "Don't know *how* the hell they *could* be any damn worse."

Sheila shook her head.

"I know it wasn't your fault, Milo. I know you been trying to turn yourself around and how good a friend you were to Jack. But it's no use. Anne already told me if you came by, not to let you in, that you're just not welcome. And you see how her father's acting."

Anne materialized out of the shadows behind her mother and pulled her by the arm back into the house.

"It's okay, Mama."

Milo could see now that there was a coterie of relatives, studying him from their vantage points on the sofa and various straight-back chairs in the gloomy living room. Sheila disappeared, and Anne and Milo stood staring at each other.

"Anne, I – "

She held up her hand to silence him. "It's no good. I don't want to hear it." She was desperately trying to hold back her tears. "Please, leave. Now."

She slowly, gently shut the door in his face.

Milo stared at it for a few seconds, then turned and walked down the steps, crossing the street and getting back into Dave's car.

Dave already had the motor running. He pulled away with a screech, but his petulant driving was the only comment he made.

Milo drifted back, remembering the last time he and Anne had gone out as a couple. It was in May of the year before he'd been inducted into the military. They hadn't been seeing each other regularly because she had been too busy at school. And she had seemed to be consciously drawing herself away from him. She had been deeply in love with him for several years, but they had been poles apart. They had wanted different things, but she'd been reluctant to admit it to herself, it just not being in the cards for them as a couple. At the time, she'd been almost done with her undergraduate work. Summer had been just around the corner. And all he'd been doing was fucking up, dealing pot for pocket change and living at his mother's.

Late one Friday afternoon, he ran into her by accident at a liquor store. He hadn't seen her in over a month. She was buying some aspirin, and he convinced her to go out with him that night.

But when he'd gone out to his car later, it wouldn't start. He fiddled with the ignition, the battery, the alternator…nothing made any difference. He was pissed off and unwilling to cancel their date.

Anne had been awarded a grant in the spring and had been getting ready to leave for a European summer study program, something that would take her right through until she began graduate school in Boston the following September.

It was one of his last chances to see her for months. On impulse, he started walking, chain-smoking, his mind churning and his fantasies running riot. He ducked into the same liquor store again and bought a pint of bourbon. When he came out on the street, he ripped off the seal and just gulped it out in the open. He spotted an unattended car, a fairly new Ford, a couple of blocks away with the windows rolled down because it was so hot. On the spur of the moment, he got in, hotwired it and jetted over to Anne's.

He was already running late, so she was outside on the porch waiting for him. He didn't shut off the motor, and they raced off in the direction of a nearby high school – already out for the summer – where they parked. Anne didn't ask about the different car, something that he later thought was odd. The sun had just gone down. Anne, for once, was in a more rebellious frame of mind, in the mood to let loose, and she helped him finish the bourbon. They talked for at least two hours, and his heart leapt; he actually started to believe that he could turn his fucked-up life in the right direction and maybe have a future with her. They got out of the car and briskly walked the track field, joking and fooling around.

The night seemed so idyllic to him in memory. Up to a certain point.

Before they returned to the car, they stripped right out in the middle of the dark, adjoining football field, both of them overwhelmed with lust for each other, and there was no hesitation as they coupled on the moist, fresh-smelling grass. After about 15 minutes, when both of them were about to come, the sprinklers went on. Instead of cooling their ardor, the warm spray excited them. Their haphazardly strewn clothes got soaked, but they didn't given a damn. Once they were done with their lovemaking, they pulled on the sopping garments, laughing.

They stopped laughing when they returned to the car.

There was a black-and-white parked sideways behind it. One cop was going through the vehicle while the other scribbled notes on a tiny pad. Milo was stunned into cruel reality, and Anne was shocked, hurt and furious. The two cops handcuffed them both, hauling them to the precinct station, and Anne had a devil of a time not being charged along with him. She was released when it became obvious to the DA's office she really had not known that the car was stolen.

Milo went to Rikers for six months. It would have been longer, except his public defender arranged a deal where he would be released with time served if he went straight into the U.S. Army. At first, he had balked at the arrangement, trying to figure the odds on from which location – Rikers or Vietnam – he would be more likely to return. Vietnam had won the coin toss. What he thought was going to be two years away metamorphosed into almost five.

Dave brought him back to the present. "You got a smoke?"

Sara was fuming, lying on her bed, one arm resting beneath her head. She chewed on a hangnail until it bled. Her bedside phone rang – a separate line from the rest of the house – and she immediately picked it up.

"Yeah."

It was Carmine. His voice was full of the same kind of anger and humiliation she felt.

"You still ready and willing to do what we talked about?"

She hesitated for only a second. "Yeah. You know I am. In a heartbeat."

"In a heartbeat? Good. I'm glad you said that, baby. We're doing it tonight. Just you an' me."

"Here at the house?"

"No, I'll tell you where later. Just be ready. Don't go off shopping."

She was in no mood for his attempts at sarcasm. "Yeah, right."

"I mean it."

"All right, already."

"Ciao."

She listlessly hung up the receiver, a stoic, unfeeling expression on her face. She thought of her mother and father, happy together when she had started first grade, and she stifled a sob.

She muttered over and over, "In a heartbeat..."

14

Marie had the unnerving sensation she was descending, not ascending, as she climbed the stairs to the Chelsea's third story. The corridor smelled. Try as she might, she couldn't identify the odor, but it was vaguely unpleasant. She walked uncertainly, studying the numbers on the doors. Finally, she stopped in front of 307, took a breath, then rapped on the heavily enameled wood.

Stefan, a fey-looking young guy with bleached-blonde hair in a lavender silk shirt and tight black jeans, opened up. God, what had she ever seen in him?

"Marie, honey! I'm glad you called. Tony didn't think you were going to make it. Get on in here, girl." He stepped aside to let her pass and closed the door. Marie didn't venture in too far. She was afraid; of what, she wasn't sure. She remained beside Stefan, looking at him, then nervously away, then back at him.

"I knew you'd come. Here, give us a kiss."

His manner had become much more affected since she'd last seen him, and she wished she hadn't called. They exchanged pecks on the cheek, and Stefan took her by the hand, leading her around the corner into the small suite. Tony was sitting on the sofa, preparing a spoonful of dope on the coffee table. Marie came to an abrupt halt, and Stefan swiveled his head to look at her.

"What's up, baby?"

Marie ignored his question, furious. "What are you doing,

Tony? I thought you were clean. I thought you were finally serious about putting some time together."

He wouldn't look at her, just continued his ritual, cooking the dope and then starting to draw it up through the cotton into a syringe.

"Stefan asked me to score 'cause the dealers know he's got more money now. 'Cause the new album's in the Top Twenty. They're always gouging him when he comes back. He said I could buy some extra – on him – so I could get high, too."

Stefan ingenuously commented. "What's the matter, honey? There's plenty for all of us. I know you're not gonna turn down some *free* shit."

Tony paused before he shot up and looked at them. "She's clean, Stefan. She's trying to get her baby back."

Stefan smoothly pulled her towards the sofa. "Oh, yeah? That's cool. You don't have to do any if you don't want to."

Tony wrapped his belt around his upper left arm, pulled it tight, then tried to find a vein.

"Yeah, Marie, just watch. We'll be done in a minute."

Marie was dismayed to actually find herself torn, not wanting to be there but unable to take her eyes off Tony's arm and the syringe. There was something alluring about the whole scenario that made her ashamed and want to puke. She let Stefan seat her on the couch. Stefan reached over and greedily grabbed a couple of packets off the table.

"You know me, I'm going to go do up mine in the bathroom." He smiled wryly. "I don't like people watchin'."

Tony had hit a vein, so he didn't look up. "Ooh, yeah, baby… sweat, sweet, sweet..." He unloosened his belt as he dislodged the rig from his arm and then licked the little dark spot of blood that appeared. "Stefan, I wouldn't do both of those at once, man. This shit is strong."

Stefan was in a hurry. "It's cool, don't worry. I got such a heavy habit now, I'll probably barely feel it and have to do a third one."

He vanished into the bathroom around the corner. Tony slumped on the sofa and threw the syringe on the table.

Marie was sweating bullets and sat there stiffly, trying to stare straight ahead.

Tony dreamily turned toward her.

"Fuck, Marie. *Relax.* Nobody's going to hold you down and make you. Shit, you don't know what you're missing. You should just do a little, it doesn't mean you're going to get strung out again."

There was a period of uncomfortable silence, Tony trying not to nod off. It was probably only a couple of minutes, but it seemed like hours. Tony scratched his cheek, then noticed the record on the table. He reached out for it with herculean effort and offered it to Marie.

"Hey, look. This is their new album."

She sneaked a glance at it just as there was a loud thud. Marie jumped, but Tony didn't notice.

"Do you think he's okay? It sounded like something fell."

Tony was oblivious, on the verge of nodding off.

Marie got up, worried, and rushed across to the bathroom door. She pressed her ear against it and knocked.

"Stefan, you okay?"

There was no response.

"Stefan, answer me."

Nothing.

Sobering a little, Tony struggled to his feet to join her. He nudged her aside and banged on the wood.

"Hey, man, you okay? What's going on in there?" He wrenched the knob, pushed on it, but the door resisted. Something was blocking it. Marie helped Tony shove. Slowly, they made some progress, revealing a pie wedge of the tiled bathroom floor and Stefan's pale blue hand.

"Oh my God!"

"Fuck!"

They frantically heaved against the door and got it open halfway. Tony stumbled in, looking down at Stefan. Suddenly he bolted past her, going for the room exit, and she latched onto his arm, yanking him back.

"What-the-fuck are you doing? We got to help him."

Tony was in a panic. "Go in there and look at him! He's beyond help. Besides I can't get caught here, high and shit. They'll revoke my probation, and I'll get a year inside."

He tore himself free and raced out of the suite and down the hall. Marie rammed her way into the bathroom and stared at Stefan's corpse. He was a pale shade of purplish blue, his eyes wide and lifeless, the syringe still in his arm. She threw the toothbrush that was in a water glass into the sink and filled the glass from the spigot, quickly splashing it onto Stefan's face. Nothing. She knelt, rolled him over and started a repeated pounding on his chest with both hands. After a minute, she listened, and she could hear nothing.

Then she panicked, too, and was running down the hall. She hit the stairway at breakneck speed and flew down it, taking three steps at a time. At the bottom, she slowed down, casually coming off the stairs into the lobby. Paranoid, she casually looked around her to see if anybody was watching.

Marie waited on the pay phone outside on the sidewalk, hoping they wouldn't take forever to answer. The ringing seemed distant, almost like it was coming from underwater. She anxiously peered at the pedestrians strolling by.

A monotone female voice came on the line. "Police emergency..."

"I want to report someone overdosing, room 307 in the Chelsea Hotel. In the bathroom. Get the paramedics there fast, it just happened..."

"Your name?"

Marie ignored the request. "You *are* gonna get somebody there right away?"

The monotone voice became annoyed. "Yeah, yeah…already typed in the call. Someone'll be there in a couple of minutes. I need your name –"

Marie slammed the phone receiver back in its cradle and hurriedly walked off.

The church was dim and deserted in the mid-afternoon light. Milo lay there on a pew towards the rear, one leg crooked and his right arm behind his head as a pillow. His eyes were closed, and he rested his bandaged left arm on his stomach. He tried to ignore the faintly nauseating smell of incense, holy water and sweat as a barrage of images crowded into his head. He wanted to blot out the picture of Jack from his mind – Jack dying in Anne's arms, the blank deadness in Jack's half-closed eyes, the expression of grief and hatred on Anne's tear-streaked face – but it seemed impossible.

He was so tired.

Disheveled Milo, his uniform in tatters, was in a smoky warehouse somewhere on the eastern outskirts of Saigon. His left arm was bleeding from MP Jerry's bullet. He could hear the murmuring of indistinct voices welling up from the shadows.

He looked down and found a swarm of poisonous vipers slithering around his feet.

Dave, smartly dressed in uniform for once, suddenly materialized in front of him.

"Man, I'm glad you were able to find this place, I was getting worried. I want you to meet these guys who're gonna help you. Just let me do the talking..."

Up ahead, Milo noticed four figures with hoods over their faces, bound and sitting in chairs before a long table.

Dave continued, lowering his voice conspiratorially, "Not them. We're framing those assholes. That's how we're getting out."

"Who are they? How come we have to frame anybody?"

Dave got annoyed. "Don't ask so many questions – "

"Who's helping us?"

"The tribunal..." Dave whispered. He turned and pointed, "...those guys."

Milo peered into the darkness. Gradually, the dingy light in the warehouse became brighter, and the figures seated on the other side of the table were revealed, all of them in military uniform: Nunzio, Carmine, Mal Powers, the Monsignor.

"Remove the penitents' hoods," Monsignor Al imperiously commanded.

Dave began tugging off the hoods, and Milo felt guilty that he wasn't surprised at their identities. Somehow, in his gut, he knew that these people would have to suffer for him. First there was Lucky, then Father Culkin, then Jack and, finally, Marie.

Without warning, Dave appeared on his left, put both of his hands on either side of Milo's head and kissed him on the mouth. When Dave moved back, Yuen stepped from the blanket of darkness on his right, his huge, silenced automatic slowly rising until it rested against the center of his forehead.

There was the loud creak of a heavy wood door closing.

The first thing Milo saw when he woke was the vaulted ceiling. He realized he was still lying in the pew.

A woman's steps echoed through the massive chamber. Mrs. Reynolds appeared walking down the main aisle, dressed in a smart, off-white ensemble with white heels and her beautiful graying blonde hair piled high. She started to pass Milo's pew, then chanced to look over and was startled.

"Oh, my lord, Milo. You gave me such a fright." She sat down in the next pew and peered down at him. "What are you doing lying there in the dark?"

He shook his head, choked up.

"What's the matter? You seem...I don't know, melancholy." He could tell she was sad, too. Her words had a slightly plaintive quality that he didn't think he'd ever heard from her before.

He changed the subject, not trusting himself to answer. "What are you doing here?

She looked away from him, staring vacantly at the altar, and sighed. "I needed to come somewhere quiet. Somewhere I felt safe. I'm...I'm rather blue today." She turned back, concerned. "Speaking of which, what's wrong, Milo?" Then she noticed the bandage. "What happened to your arm?"

"Not much, it'll be all right." He hesitated. "My best friend was killed last night."

"Oh, no..." she said softly, "I'm so sorry."

He smiled sadly at her. "And why are you blue?"

"Oh, no, I'd feel a fool to mention it now. My problem doesn't compare -- "

"No, go on, I want to know. I can tell something's wrong."

She paused, then feigned a laugh. "My husband's leaving me. Fancy that. Wants a divorce."

Milo slowly sat up. "Why?"

She gave him a knowing look. "Really, Milo. Can't you guess?"

He grasped her hand from where she had it draped along the pew. "I'm sorry."

"It's all right. It actually *wasn't* you. I was with somebody else uptown. Harold had me followed by a private detective. It's all so sordid." She laughed. "I was seen several times, out with this man… you know, the man the detective saw. The thing is, this male friend of mine is *gay.*" She laughed louder at the irony of it, but grew self-conscious as her voice reverberated off the walls. Putting trembling fingers to her mouth, she shot him a mischievous look, then leaned over, spontaneously clasping his fingers to her lips and kissing his hand. For a fleeting few seconds, Milo fought the impulse to take her in his arms. He felt a deep love for this woman, who, all at once, seemed so much like a young girl. But he instinctively knew there was nothing he could say to make things right.

A tear ran down her cheek.

"I just wish I knew what I was going to do. You see, he made me sign, what do they call it these days? I believe it's a pre-nuptial agreement." She stood up and gave him a bitter smile. "I really should be going…I'm due at the lawyer's."

She started to walk away, then stopped. "I'm very sorry about your friend."

He smiled. “Thank you, Dorrie.”

“And thanks, Milo. Thank you for always being so sweet to me.”

Her footsteps echoed loudly as she turned and walked down the aisle. When she pushed open the doors, she cut a fine, dignified figure, silhouetted against the setting sun.

Milo’s heart ached.

As Milo approached his room, he could see that the door was ajar, so he carefully swung it open, dreading what new landmine might have been set for him. But it was Marie, lying on his cot.

He sat down beside her, and she awoke with a start. He smoothed her hair back out of her face.

“You okay?”

She seemed as if she’d been crying. “Hi, Milo.” For almost thirty seconds she seemed unable to speak. “I don’t know if I am okay.” She hesitated again. “I saw someone OD today. Someone I knew from my past.”

Then she saw the bandage. “Jesus! What happened? You weren’t at the center last night, were you? You heard about that? Father Culkin getting killed?

Milo nodded. “This…” he held up his arm, “…happened later.” He stood up and walked to the window, not looking at her. “Marie, I’ve got to camp out somewhere else for a few days. You should go back to your sober living and stay put.”

“Where are you going?”

He looked at her. “I don’t think it would be a good idea for you to know.”

She stood and went to him. “I don’t know what’s going on, Milo, but I’m not going anywhere till you at least let me know where you’re gonna be.”

He shook his head and stared back out the window.

She tugged at his sleeve. “I mean it.”

He didn’t say anything right away. Finally, exasperated but resigned, he turned, took her hand and led her out of the room.

Carmine, looking grim, and Yuen, ambivalent, strode briskly toward Fiorille restaurant. Carmine happened to idly glance across the street and was greeted by a sight he could have done without. Smiling Fed O’Reilly was propped against his unmarked car, sipping a cup of coffee. He gave a cheerful wave.

Rizzo sat sulkily by himself at a booth in the restaurant, nursing a beer, with an untouched plate of spaghetti in front of him. There were sounds of the bell on the entrance, then coins noisily dropping into the jukebox and finally a mournful old ballad sung in Italian at low volume.

Carmine stopped beside the table. "Nice of you to finally show up somewhere."

Rizzo timidly answered, "I had a rough night."

Carmine's temper rose. "Really? A rough night. That's what you call it?"

Rizzo was too scared to look at him.

"So…where's Gino?"

Rizzo finally made eye contact, nervously wiping his mouth on a napkin.

"Uh...he's not around."

"Yeah? Is that right?" Carmine's voice dripped with vitriolic sarcasm. "I hear he's not around *anywhere anymore*."

Anatoli suddenly materialized from the kitchen, but as soon as he caught sight of Carmine and the expression on Rizzo's face, he did an about-face and disappeared.

Rizzo was starting to shake. "Oh, so you heard..."

"Yeah, I heard. Along with every-other-fucking-body in New York who watches TV and reads the papers."

"I was going to tell you but – "

Furious, Carmine swept the plate and glass into Rizzo's lap.

"But what, Rizzo? What lies are you going to tell me now?"

Rizzo flushed bright red. Carmine slapped him hard on the back of the head.

"Moron! Fucking moron!"

Customers in the front part of the restaurant turned to stare. Carmine immediately noticed them and spun around. "What the fuck are you looking at? Is this any of your business?"

The maître d' came over to the two couples at the front table, talking to them in low, conciliatory tones.

Rizzo scrambled to put a positive spin on his debacle. "We found out who's been ripping off the dealers, Carmine."

Carmine lowered his voice, calming down. "I heard."

Rizzo gave him a questioning stare, and Carmine wagged his head at the front. Rizzo twisted his neck to look and saw Yuen leaning against the cash register, chewing a toothpick, with his arms folded.

Rizzo turned his attention back to Carmine, then gazed

shamefully down at his wet lap.

Carmine jammed a finger in Rizzo's chest. "It would've been nice if you could've found out about the guys hijacking the dealers without getting one of our crew killed. And, even worse, having it make the goddamn papers. You should have taken Gino's body with you."

"I know, I know."

"You've got more brains than that. At least I thought you did."

Rizzo became defensive. "I was just trying to get Anatoli out of there alive. Once we left, and I realized we'd left Gino, it was too late. Cops were crawlin' all over the fuckin' place."

At last, Carmine sat down, looked over at the waiter, grabbed Rizzo's empty beer bottle and wagged it at him. He looked back at Rizzo and sighed melodramatically. The waiter brought him a beer and a glass, then poured it for him.

Carmine threw Rizzo a napkin. "Clean yourself up... so where is the kid?"

Rizzo gave him a puzzled look.

Carmine sipped the beer. "The kid, Anatoli."

Rizzo gestured towards the kitchen. "He's in the back somewheres."

"Cops been around yet, askin' questions? Those fuckin' Feds?"

Rizzo stood so he could more easily dab at his soiled trouser front.

"No Feds. One cop came by. That dumb homicide dick, Taliaferro. We're lucky it was him. I told him I hadn't seen Gino since yesterday afternoon. I'm pretty sure he believed me."

"We'll see, won't we? None of those cops are as stupid as you think, even if they do occasionally take dough." Carmine pointed a threatening finger. "You guys are goin' out tonight to look for those two mooks who've been knockin' over the dealers." He gestured towards Yuen. "Take him with you. He knows both of them from before, from fuckin' Vietnam of all places. He's a crack shot. It'll be a sure thing if you get lucky and spot 'em."

Rizzo nodded.

Yuen studied the pair from the corner of his eye, disgusted. Never before had he had to work with such cretins. He swiveled his body, pushing off from the cashier's station, leaning forward onto the brass rail that ran crossways in the middle of Fiorille's enormous front window. He casually lit a cigarette and watched the redheaded Fed across the street gabbing with his partner. He had decided to catch a plane back to Macao as soon as he had eliminated Milo and Dave, whether his business with Carmine was finished or not.

15

Milo felt horribly distracted, pulled in too many directions at once. Marie had to hurry along to keep up with him as he walked. Infuriated, she grabbed onto his arm.

"Look, you know what? I don't give a damn where you're staying if you don't want me to know."

He stared at the sidewalk for a few seconds as he caught his breath, then looked into her eyes. "Marie, you have to understand. This has nothing to do with you or my feelings for you. Some heavy shit is going down, and I'm right in the middle of it."

She was confused. "How?"

"It's a long, stupid story. I just saw someone die, too. Last night. In fact, I saw several people die...violently. One of them was my best friend. And his wife, who I've been friends with since high school, blames me." He paused and dreamily squinted into the sinking sun. "She's probably right."

Marie was embarrassed. "I'm sorry, Milo. I didn't realize...I was already freaked out because I might get kicked out of my sober living. The stupid chick who runs the place saw the two of us together, and she gave me hell. She's supposed to let me know tonight if I can stay. She wanted to 'think it over.' If she decides I have to go, I'll have no place to live. I don't know what'll happen with my little girl. It'll be a big step backwards."

"Marie, the place I'm going right now is in the South Bronx.

It's a hairy place. Really hairy."

"I've been in the South Bronx before, Milo. I used to fucking smoke crack."

He grabbed her and held her to his chest. She slowly raised her arms to clasp his back.

Dave drew aside the flimsy curtain from his window and peered down to the street. Five floors down, Milo and Marie were crossing the deserted thoroughfare. Dave let the curtain fall in place and shook his head, annoyed.

"Fucking dumbbell."

Downstairs, Milo paused at the big double glass doors of the old building.

"I'll be up on the fifth floor. It's the only loft in the place that's not vacant. My friend's name is Dave." He stopped, unsure of how much more he should tell her. "Just so you know, if you stop by and I'm not around...he's kind of an asshole."

She smiled and stood on her tiptoes to kiss him quickly on the cheek.

"If some shit comes down at your sober living, meet me here later. Dave and I may go out, but we'll be back. You can wait here in the lobby." He handed her a key. "This is to the front lobby doors. Dave loaned it to me. He's got another. If homeless guys look like they're going to start trying to get in to sleep it off or shoot up," he gestured inside into the foyer, "Push that desk over there up against the doors. But I doubt that'll happen, and I don't think we'll be out late."

Marie nodded. "Hopefully I won't see you again till tomorrow."

"Be careful going back. You know what train to take, right?"

She nodded.

As an afterthought, Milo pulled out a pen and a piece of paper to scrawl on. "Listen, take a cab if you need to come back here. Most taxis won't come to this neighborhood anymore." He handed her the paper. "But these two guys, Angel and Ahmet, have gypsy cabs. They're cool. Tell them I gave you their numbers. If they don't answer, Angel hangs out a lot at the corner café down the street from Green Pastures."

She smiled.

They reached out to each other by instinct, touched fingertips, then she started walking backwards into the late afternoon sun, trying to blink away tears.

Milo waited patiently as the antique freight elevator climbed, carrying him to Dave's loft. At last, it noisily bucked to a halt. He pulled the door up vertically to open it.

Dave stood there with his arms folded, leaning against the wall.

"You think it's wise she knows where we are?"

Milo gave him a frustrated look, shook his head and walked to the center of the big room.

Dave was getting worked up. "Think a minute, hotshot. Haven't those guinea bastards seen her with you?"

Dave had a point. He, himself, knew she should be kept in the dark, and now he remembered why he had had that gut feeling. But he'd already caved, unable to keep anything from her.

"Yeah, right! You forgot about those pricks givin' her shit in the crosswalk the other day."

"They don't know where she's staying," he claimed, trying to reassure himself as well as Dave. "They don't know her name. I'm certain of it."

Dave strolled to his work table by the window. "You better hope not. 'Cause they're gonna be out lookin'. And not just for me. You better say a prayer they don't run across her."

"So before all that shit broke loose at Culkin's last night, what were you up to? What was that thing Sugar said? About you heisting dealers?"

Dave waxed smugly philosophical. "A man's gotta make a living. I didn't take anybody's money who didn't deserve to have it taken."

Milo sat down on the windowsill. "And you didn't whack anybody who didn't deserve to get whacked."

"Don't worry." Dave was so fucking sure of himself. "We take care of a few loose ends, and we'll be okay."

Milo leaned his head against the dirty pane of glass. "I don't know why I'm surprised."

Dave casually changed the subject. "How's the arm?"

Milo glanced at his bandaged limb as if he'd forgotten about it.

"Better let me change the dressing. You don't want to let it get infected."

He reached into a canvas bag under the table and withdrew a roll of bandages, hydrogen peroxide, cotton and Qtips. He then quickly walked over to the sink protruding from the wall and scrubbed his hands with powdered soap and water. Milo carefully unwrapped the bandage. Dave crouched down beside him, examining the wound like an expert. He daubed hydrogen peroxide liberally on a wad of cotton, then poured a stream of it over the bullethole in Milo's forearm.

"Fuck!"

"It actually looks okay. Man, you're lucky it went clean through." He swiftly wound a fresh bandage to tightly cover the now cotton-covered wound. He laughed. "Hey, man, that's a trip and a half seeing Yuen over here, hunh? Who would've thought after all these years, all those thousands of miles between us? Him in bed with the goddamn mob. Dope brings all kinds of wonderful people together."

"I can't believe he's still alive."

Dave eased down into the chair, put the bandages and peroxide away, then pulled out another automatic from the canvas bag. He lovingly placed it on the table next to the one already resting there in pieces.

"I never asked you back then, because I didn't want to know. You framed him for Lucky and Jerry, didn't you?"

Dave started to dismantle the second gun, ignoring the question.

"Goddamn it, Dave. Answer me."

Once he was done, Dave moved his hands to the other one and quickly began re-assembling it.

"You fucking pussy! Sure I did. Why not? He was already ripping us off behind our backs, cutting the shit more than he had any right to. And he did it as much 'cause you were boning his sister as for the money. He hated our fucking guts. Grow up already. You still don't know how the real world works."

"Teach me, Dave. I already know you will, whether I want you to or not."

Dave cheerfully switched gears. "This actually worked out fine. Made everything come to a head."

"Yeah, you asshole. Jack and Culkin fucking murdered. Worked out just fucking fine."

"What do you think would have happened if I hadn't butted in?"

"They would have thrown a good scare into us. They were stupid, but not that stupid. They wouldn't have killed anyone."

"Best outcome – at the very least, Culkin would have ended up in the hospital."

Milo glared at him. "You were the one who had to shoot first, kill Sugar when he recognized you."

Dave ignored him. "If I don't miss my guess, Nunzio's on the way out, and Carmine's on the way in. Everything I hear on the street is pointing that way. That guy I know, O'Reilly, from Justice? The one who's on stakeout across from their restaurant? He tells me basically the same thing. Some shit's gonna go down…soon. Now that you're not staying at the church, it's a perfect opportunity to hit Nunzio's little treasure chamber."

"You're fucking nuts."

Dave's face dissolved into a shit-eating grin. "I know, but I'm having so much fucking fun."

Not feeling that he had any other viable options, Milo was resigned. "I guess I don't have any choice if I want to come up with dough to get out of this town."

"Now you're talkin'." He slammed a bullet clip into the automatic and handed it to Milo. "We're on for tonight."

Milo handed back the weapon. "No guns. Not inside the church."

Dave looked at him as if he was crazy. He shook his head, grabbed inside the canvas bag and came out with a sheathed buck knife, which he slapped down on the table. "Fine."

Slightly drunk, Nunzio stumbled into the vestibule, then down into the long, winding darkness of the stone stairway to the cellars. He was too lazy to go to the circuit-breaker box and turn the stair lights on. About halfway down, in that enveloping blackness, a cold shiver ran down his spine, and he stopped to keep his balance.

"What-the-fuck?" he thought, "What-the-hell's happening to me lately? Am I drinking too much? My liver doesn't bounce back like it did when I was in my forties." But it wasn't just that, it was everything. He'd gone through all kinds of catastrophes with the law, with rivals, with psycho "associates" who didn't know their place. He'd weathered hellacious turf wars where scores had fallen. This thing with the candy-ass storefront rehab was nothing. It was something else. He'd gone too far with Carmine. He'd realized it right away, the second he'd first banged his head into the fridge. But he hadn't been able to stop. His anger had been at a boiling point and wouldn't come back down.

Everything that had been going on those last couple of years, it was eating away at his insides. Al would say his "soul." Living with the memory of Andrea. Living with the ever-growing hatred of Sara. Yeah, strangely enough, when he was drunk, he could admit it to himself.

That girl, his own flesh and blood, hated his goddamned guts. And so did Carmine, he could tell. But Jesus, he wasn't in some kind of popularity contest. He had to run a tight, brutal ship. He had to be harder than anyone else around him, or his fiefdom would disintegrate. He didn't hold with some of the wizened antics of the supposedly generous, older bosses who'd turned their territories over to comparatively younger blood. That was bullshit. "Fuck it," he thought, "I'm okay. I'm just going through a phase. I'll ease up on the drinking, get a couple more hours sleep a night. I'll be fine, and these heebie-jeebies will blow over."

When he got to the bottom, he squinted into the dim light thrown by the one 40-watt bulb that hung at the mouth of the corridor. Once he was in front of the door to his treasure chamber, he fumbled for the right key. He had so many, he couldn't find it right away, and he muttered profane oaths under his breath.

"Goddamn it," he lamented, whispering to himself, "Nothing is fucking going right." Then he laughed. "Jeez, I really am getting – what you call it? – neurotic in my old age."

He turned the key, wrenched the doorknob and pushed. The door swung open, and he switched on the anemic overhead fluorescent light. It wouldn't fully come on, giving off eerie strobe flickers that put his nerves on edge. What looked like cigarette smoke was visibly spiraling up from the back of Nunzio' favorite throne-like chair.

"What-the-fuck?"

Two black leather-clad woman's legs materialized in front of it.

Nunzio was shocked and angry. "How the hell did you get in here?"

All at once, as she stood, he realized it was Sara, her hair up, and her svelte body clad in a black turtleneck and leather pants. She stubbed out her cigarette and smiled.

"Hi, Papa."

He reached out for her. "Why, you fucking little bitch!"

Just as Nunzio was about to connect with his hand, an arm encircled his neck from behind in a taut chokehold, and Carmine's demonic face loomed over his left shoulder. Suddenly, Nunzio was terrified.

"What-the-hell's going on – ?"

He tried to twist around to see who it was. Then Carmine's right hand was descending with a straight razor, drawing it across and slitting his boss's throat. Blood geysered from his neck. Sara homed in on her father's chest, stabbing him in the heart with his own jeweled, antique dagger.

Carmine whispered in Nunzio's ear. "Ciao, Padrino."

Milo, in blue denim jacket and jeans, and Dave, clad in black, wound their way along the church perimeter in the diredction of the rear driveway that separated the church from the rectory. There was the sputtering roar of a revved-up engine, and a van catapulted out onto the street. They both recognized the figures inside – Sara in the passenger seat and Carmine at the wheel.

Dave cursed. "Shit!"

"I'm getting a bad feeling."

"Really?" Dave sarcastically asked. "Then we'd better get the fuck in there."

Dave and Milo stealthily made their way inside and loped down the steps to the basement level. As they approached the open treasure chamber door, Dave motioned to Milo to stay put, but Milo continued on with him, stopping just before they reached the entrance.

He recognized Monsignor Al's sobbing voice. "Jeez, Dom, why? Why?"

They both peered into the chamber. Monsignor Aloysius came into view, sitting on the floor with Nunzio's head cradled in his lap under the cold, creepy harshness of the fluorescent light. He caressed Nunzio's ashen face. The room was now totally empty except for a golden candelabra overturned on the floor.

"Do you understand now?" The Monsignor whispered. "This is the kind of thing I was afraid of....oh, sweet Jesus!"

Dave grimaced with disgust, backed up and gestured for Milo to follow him.

Once they were on the street again, the two of them settled into a brisk walk.

"My timing was completely off. I saw something like this coming, but not so goddamn fucking fast. Christ! The guy's own daughter helped to do him, can you believe that?"

"Nothing like the Mafia for the sick family shit."

"I'd already figured she hated his guts. You know, don't you, that that sick fuck, Nunzio, drove his wife – Sara's mother – off her rocker? He basically killed her."

"And where does Carmine come in?"

"I'd figured Sara was balling him. I'd seen the two of them together once when I was tailing him. All cozy. I'd guessed Carmine would convince her to help double cross the old man. Still – Jesus H. Christ on the cross -- I thought he wouldn't pull anything this soon."

"Nunzio must've blown a gasket when he heard about the massacre at Green Pastures. I'd lay odds he didn't know Rizzo and Mal were going to roust Culkin. That's not his style, teaming up with a black guy."

"It's my own fucking fault. I was pushing the buttons too quick. Fucking goddamn it! You just wait, though. I know how to fix these motherfuckers."

"How?"

"I'll just have to work some of my magic. Like in Nam. Remember the Laotian colonel, his slut wife and the VC rat?"

Milo stopped walking, and Dave impatiently looked back at him, hovering at the lip of a narrow alley.

"Shit, Dave. That's crazy."

Dave smiled. "No, it's not. Almost the same damn thing."

The pair didn't notice a black Cadillac sedan was coming down the street toward them with its lights off.

Jumpy Anatoli was at the wheel. Rizzo became excited like a little kid at the sight of the two men ahead, and he fidgeted in the front passenger seat, unable to sit still. Yuen calmly leaned out the driver's side rear window with his silenced automatic. The car slowed to a creepy-crawl.

"Fuck!" Dave abruptly spotted them and jumped in front of Milo. Immediately, there was a quick succession of muffled shots, and Dave collapsed, riddled with lead. He toppled onto Milo, knocking him horizontal in the alley driveway.

A barely detectable smile of satisfaction spread across Yuen's face as he saw Dave fall. A wailing siren cut in from down the street. Yuen glanced behind the car.

Rizzo twisted round, and Anatoli adjusted the rear view to see the police cruiser homing in on them. Anatoli floored it, and Rizzo angrily slapped him on the back of his head.

"You ass! You just spotting them now?"

Milo watched the black sedan and the pursuing cruiser whip around the next street corner, brakes squealing and tires screeching. He struggled out from under Dave and sat up, propping Dave's head in his lap. All at once, the images of Anne with Jack and Monsignor Al with Nunzio popped unbidden and unwelcome into his brain.

Dave's mumbled words were punctuated with a gurgling sound. "Wow, I always wondered what I'd do..."

"Dave -- "

"--you know what I mean? If it was like...a split second thing... whether it meant me...or the other guy...gettin' it -- " He coughed blood. "Now I know."

Milo started to get up, and he put his hands under Dave's arms, trying to help him stand. "I've got to get you to a doctor."

Dave laughed, but it changed into a coughing fit. "Man, you are a scream. Don't make me regret I stepped in front of you."

Milo relaxed and sat back down, hugging his friend. Dave pushed him away.

"Listen to me, you dumb ass. You got to get out of here... now..." Blood streamed copiously from his lips. "...just remember, though...'cause you're gonna…have to be the one to do it now...the Laotian colonel and his bitch. Same thing...Carmine, Sara and Mal... just think before – "

Dave suddenly couldn't catch his breath. He tried to touch Milo's face, but it was too far to reach, and he died.

Milo gently laid him out on the pavement. He slowly stood, teetering as if he'd had the wind knocked out of him, and he stared down at his dead friend.

He was starting to have one of his spells. He was seeing things that he knew weren't there. The building on the other side of the alley looked exactly like the U.S. Embassy compound in Saigon, that day of the bombing. He blinked. It wouldn't go away. He had to start walking. He turned down the alley, picking his way amongst the bomb victims' dismembered limbs and the slick pools of blood. He had to pause again, and he leaned against the alley wall in the shadow of a fire escape. Anxiety amped up the colors in his retinas. The shadows went lavender, and the cold street lights at either end of the alley changed to a blood red and a painful, nauseating yellow.

Ten blocks away in a residential neighborhood, the pursuit was still going, hot and heavy. Yuen casually leaned out the back window, shooting at the cops. One of his bullets connected with the driver, and the black-and-white veered out of control, smashing into a row of parked cars.

Rizzo was overjoyed. But Yuen remained his stoic self, settling back and refastening his seat belt.

Rizzo laughed. "All right! Like shooting fish in a fucking barrel!"

Anatoli was rattled, his brain overloaded, dense with a fog of confusion caused by the sudden let-up of tension. If Rizzo had been more perceptive, he would have seen from the dazed expression on the kid's face that something was wrong.

A delivery truck came out of nowhere, and Anatoli swerved to miss it. The sedan stood up on its driver-side wheels and crashed head-on into the traffic signal on the southwest corner. It came to rest on its side and miraculously didn't turn all the way over.

Yuen easily extricated himself from the passenger side rear window and jumped to the pavement. He nonchalantly wiped a trickle of blood from his forehead, examined it dispassionately, then withdrew a handkerchief from his suit and wiped his hands. He drifted over to stand in front of the car, and he looked down at the windshield.

Anatoli was panicking as he realized that Rizzo – his best friend, his cousin and protector – was dead. Scrambling and clawing at the bloody upholstery, trying to climb out from under Rizzo's body, he gave off mewling, whimpering sounds of agony. As he tried to open the passenger side door, he stepped on Rizzo's face.

Yuen impassively watched him, indifferent to the man's need for help and to the few bystanders from the neighborhood that were starting to cluster around. Another siren welled up out of the darkness.

Anatoli became angry when he saw Yuen staring at him. "Fuck, man. Help me!"

Yuen stoically, slowly moved to the side of the car and helped Anatoli climb down. Then he started to walk away. Anatoli shamefacedly followed him.

One of the bystanders, an old, bald-headed man in a T-shirt and pajama bottoms, tried to get their attention, waving at them with a rolled-up newspaper.

"Hey! Hey, you guys! The cops are gonna want to talk to you. Your friend got killed. You can't leave the scene of an accident."

Anatoli turned as he stalked away, his old bravado returning. "Oh, yeah?" he sneered. "Watch us."

16

By the time Milo got back to Dave's place, the sun was starting to rise on the other side of the buildings behind him. Having one of his spells, then trying to cast off the wave of hallucinations, had made him forget Dave's Cougar was parked a few blocks from the cathedral. If he'd remembered, he could have driven, but he'd ended up walking the whole way, fighting demons, taking him forever.

He paused as he spotted someone in the shadowy space behind the beat-up desk in the disused lobby. Then he realized it was Marie, dozing with her head against the wall. She felt his eyes on her as he came in, and she jumped.

"Why did you leave this unlocked?"

"Shit! I'm sorry. I fell asleep."

He didn't say anything.

"You okay?" She saw Dave's blood on his jeans and put her hand to her mouth. "Oh my God."

He sat down beside her, but offered no explanation for his appearance.

She stared at him for a minute while she collected her thoughts and tried to ignore the blood. "That bitch kicked me out of sober living as soon as I got back there. But I found a job last night in Manhattan. This bookstore called Arcane Encounter."

Milo swallowed and fought back images of Jack's blood spurting all over Anne and the scattered books on their living-room floor.

"The owner said he lost his assistant manager. I start next Monday."

Somehow Milo maintained a poker face. He didn't want to have to explain to her who she was replacing at the bookstore. "I'm glad you got a job."

She went on, "I tried going upstairs but didn't get an answer. Where's your friend, Dave?"

"He's dead."

Marie was speechless.

He reached out his hand to her and pulled her to her feet as he stood.

"Let's go up."

The curtains were pulled across the windows in Dave's loft, but the sunlight seeped around the borders. Milo and Marie sat in the shadows on a sleeping bag below one of the ledges and shared a cigarette.

"I don't understand. Did this Vietnamese guy come here to New York looking for you two? Or was it just a coincidence?"

"I don't know. He's the kind that doesn't forget if someone has fucked him over."

"Which Dave definitely did."

"As far as he's concerned, we both did. Somehow, I don't think he knew ahead of time we were here in New York. He's always been involved with drugs, moving big quantities since the early Seventies while the war was still on. I have a feeling he came here specifically to meet up with Carmine. And we just crossed paths by chance."

They sat quietly for a few seconds.

"Fuck," she whispered.

"I don't really know what I'm going to do about him. But I've got an idea how to handle Carmine and Mal. Something Dave was originally planning in that twisted brain of his. Before Yuen shot him."

"Why can't we just get out of New York?"

"It won't work unless I can take them all down first. Eventually, someone would catch up to us."

"But why Carmine and Mal, too?"

Milo tried to keep his patience, explaining all the details to her. "Because they think I was in on it with Dave, ripping off the dealers. An idea I'm sure Yuen was only too happy to encourage."

Marie lay down, resting her head on his thigh.

"I'm going to help you."

"No."

"Yes." She reached out to clasp his right hand and squeezed it. "You can't do it all by yourself."

Milo didn't talk anymore. The sounds of traffic, the city coming awake, filtered up from the streets five floors below.

"Let's get some rest. We'll start tomorrow morning, bright and early."

She lay there beside Milo on the sleeping bag, but couldn't sleep. Surprisingly, he had dropped right off, emotionally and physically drained. She was, too, and maybe if it hadn't been for her thoughts of Rimi, she could have made a quick exit into dreamland. Dreamland – all she had lately were bad dreams. Dreams of toddling Rimi not remembering her. Dreams of Rimi as a grown-up teenager finding Marie's bright-blue, OD'ed corpse, Rimi then being so disgusted that she had wadded up her mother's body like a foul, soiled piece of cloth and had thrown it in a Dumpster. How could she ever get Rimi back now, getting kicked out of sober living? The conditions of her probation were unalterable.

Once all the nightmarish violence had at last come to an end, she needed to remember to call Aggie, her caseworker. Actually, she *couldn't* wait that long. It might be days. She needed to call her immediately, if not sooner. She was sure Aggie would understand. They'd done a test on her at the house right before kicking her out – Marie had insisted on it – and she came up clean. But they booted her anyway. At least she had it on record. That should mean something. And after having resisted the urge at the Chelsea, descending into hell with Stefan and Tony – something only Tony knew about. After all that, she was sure she wouldn't pick up. What better aversion therapy could there be?

Fraternizing with Milo, especially since he was several years clean, couldn't be that big a deal, could it? She was in love with Milo, and she was certain somehow they could make a future together.

But then again, the legal bureaucrats would not think that way. Aggie, too, even if she understood, might have to toe the line and violate her. Father Culkin would likely have interceded on her behalf, but he was dead.

All at once, she realized she was getting way ahead of herself. This worrying about what was years, months, even just weeks down the line, and the panic attacks it set off, was what had always sparked her binges before – smoking crack and meth and heroin to get out of herself and shut off the paranoid voices in her brain. But they made the voices worse. She looked over at Milo and thought, “I’m okay right now. I have someone I love beside me. Someone who cares for me and loves me, too. I am lucky. I’m not sleeping on the street. Somehow, things will work out.” Before she knew it, she had dozed off.

Milo was back at Green Pastures, sleeping upstairs in the spartan guest room that Culkin sometimes used for drying-out drunks or kicking junkies, unfortunates who had no other place to go. He was lying with Marie on a bare mattress on the hardwood floor when two men climbed through the window that overlooked the back alley. The men were on the far end of the room and didn’t seem to notice them. They looked like a couple of the stooges that Milo had seen with Rizzo one time, but he didn’t know their names. Milo repeatedly nudged Marie to wake her, but she wouldn’t stir. He looked away for a second to see if the hallway door to the stairs was open, but when he turned back, the men had disappeared.

The sounds of an AA meeting in progress wafted up from the first floor. He stood and pulled on his shoes, and made his way halfway down the kitchen staircase to see how many people were there. It was packed. He was surprised to see various alcoholics and addicts acting out their life stories in skits, and he thought to himself, “What a novel idea.” He couldn’t remember ever having been at a meeting like that before.

A scream from the guest room interrupted his reverie, and he jumped back up the steps three at a time, frightened that Rizzo’s men had returned and were victimizing Marie. When he burst through the door, he saw he was too late. One of the men was disappearing out the window with an unconscious Marie slung over his shoulder, like in an old movie serial. He raced to the opening to stare after them, but they’d already disappeared down the alley. Suddenly he heard a door open, and he whirled to find two more men creeping out of a closet behind him, their claw-like hands poised to grab. To their surprise, he jumped into their arms, and the trio crashed to the floor, rolling about in a confusion of limbs.

Milo felt nauseous and, closing his eyes for a few seconds to clear his head, he was greeted by an astonishing sight when he reopened them. The two men had changed into alligators, and he had to leap to his feet to avoid their snapping jaws. Somehow he caught one by the tail and, possessed of a herculean strength, he twirled it around and around, then let it go, slinging it like a discus out the open window, down, down, down into the rear alley. Relieved that he'd gotten rid of one, he wasn't prepared for the cruel surprise in store for him as the other one welded its jaws around his waist. He soundlessly cried out and tried to wrench himself free. The mighty teeth held him fast, piercing his stomach and kidneys, and when he glanced back into the room, he was confronted with a horrifying vision. It was Lucky's room in Saigon. She and Jerry, both dead and drenched in blood, lay on the bare mattress. He noticed Jerry's .45 lying at their feet, so he tumbled to the floor, with the alligator still attached to his midriff. He stretched himself with an exhausting effort so he could almost touch the weapon. He scrambled another couple of inches and took it in his palm. The gun was unbelievably heavy. Nevertheless, he promptly raised it, pressed it to the head of the gigantic reptile, then squeezed the trigger. A muffled, wet pop sounded, and the beast died. Milo rolled from its jaws and, leaving a trail of blood and viscera, he crawled in agony to the window. Outside, there it was -- the lavender sky, the blood red bats and Saigon's slum district skyline.

He woke in a cold sweat. Slowly opening his eyes, he found Marie with her head on the right side of his chest, drowsily nuzzling into the crook of his arm. The sleeping bag felt damp and clammy under him. He looked at his watch and saw that it was already 5:00 AM. They'd made love a few times, and he figured, even allowing for that, they'd been sleeping off and on for almost 13 hours.

17

Milo finished his conversation on the payphone, then hung it up. Marie stood there beside him, propping open the folding door. Milo took hold of her hand, and they hurried across the street.

Outside Nunzio's house, a group of men, all clad in black suits and sunglasses, milled around on the sidewalk, talking in low, somber tones. Five black sedans were lined up at the curb.

Gus, looking grief-stricken, came out the front door, put on sunglasses after wiping his eyes with his handkerchief and then joined the cluster of men. Sara came out after him, also clad in mourning garb, and she shut the door behind her.

Carmine's red Lincoln Continental, with the top up, slowly cruised down the narrow street from the direction of the main avenue. A 50-ish, thick-set underboss from the Bronx named Rosso was holding forth from the back seat.

"Don't worry, Carmine. We're gonna find out who did this, fuckin' scumbag bastards."

Carmine made no comment as he slowed the car to a crawl, just nodding in reply to the vengeful sentiments. Scarpelli, an older, thinner boss from Queens, with a thick mane of greying hair, sat in the front passenger seat and chimed in.

"Ten-to-one it was that no-good Zingarelli. He and Dom were fightin' for months over the stadium concessions. I heard him sayin' myself just last month, 'Nunzio! You're gonna regret this!'"

Suddenly, Carmine spotted something ahead that made him

brake. The other two stared, open-mouthed.

Sara was fidgeting at the bottom of the steps with a sour expression on her face when Mal Powers appeared out of nowhere with a huge bouquet of flowers. He was obviously expressing his condolences. Sara awkwardly smiled and accepted the flowers.

Gus did a double take as he saw Mal. He zeroed in on him, but he was on the other side of the small bunch of men, so he had to elbow through to get to Sara.

"Jesus H. Christ!" Scarpelli exclaimed. He glanced questioningly at Rosso, then at Carmine.

Rosso scooted forward. "What's with the *moolignon*? You know him, Carmine?"

Carmine was speechless, his face flushed with anger.

Marie was sitting on the curb three houses down on the other side. She watched the melodrama unfolding, and she desperately tried not to laugh as the morbidly obese Gus hustled the indignant Mal into his waiting cab. After another few seconds, all the men on the sidewalk piled into the sedans. Sara stepped into Carmine's Lincoln as it pulled up, and then the cortege quickly rolled away.

The cars passed Marie, but she waited until they'd disappeared around the corner before moving. She ran down the block and stopped directly across from the Nunzio driveway. She cautiously glanced back and forth on the street to make sure no one was watching her, then waved.

Milo was behind Nunzio's house at the end of the drive, peering around the rear corner by the kitchen porch. He acknowledged Marie's signal, then swiftly jumped up on the porch to huddle in front of the door lock. He had a set of burglar picks, and it only took him a couple of minutes to gain access.

Once inside, he furtively made his way through the kitchen and into the living room. He was alert for any noises, unsure if he was truly alone in the house. He paused at the bottom of the stairs for a full minute, listening, then slowly climbed the steps. At the top, he got his bearings, then walked down the hall, quietly opening each door that he passed.

He immediately recognized Sara's room from its decor, and he carefully made his way into and around the room, searching for anything appropriate he could take. He nimbly eased open a chest of drawers and began to go through her underwear. Something caught his eye – a transparent bra, made of sheer fabric with a distinctive, recognizable rose-bloom pattern on the straps. Stuffing it inside his denim jacket, he continued to inspect the room, but he found nothing else that interested him, so he left.

Milo rapidly descended the stairs, and he was about to return to the kitchen when he spotted some photo albums sitting on the coffee table by the television. He picked one up, quickly paged through it, set it down, then picked up another. He stopped as he found the photo that he wanted: Sara in a provocative bikini. He was surprised her father had let it be inserted in the family album. With a delicate touch, he removed the snapshot from its slot and tucked it inside his jacket, then set the book back on the table.

Marie was now sitting on the curb directly across the street, nervously scanning the block. All seemed quiet, but still she fretted, wondering if any of the neighbors who might be at home were particularly friendly with the Nunzio family.

Milo was in the kitchen, about to leave, when he noticed the basement door. He tried to open it, but it was locked. Quickly, his burglar tools reappeared in his hands, and he knelt to pick the lock. After an anxious minute, it clicked, and he easily rotated the knob. He switched on the light at the top of the steep, narrow steps and started down.

At the bottom, there was more darkness. Milo groped on the wall, found a switch and flipped it on.

The entire haul from Nunzio's treasure chamber was revealed, sitting there before him. Spotting a large, empty canvas bag on a filthy work table, Milo grabbed it and began to fill it with various pieces of jewelry, gold and art objects that were small enough to easily fit. As an afterthought, he picked up a small painting that seemed the work of an old master and awkwardly stuffed it in the bag.

Once he was in the kitchen again, he was cautious to leave the basement door in the same locked condition as he had found it.

Outside, he stood close to the wall of the house with the bag, and he peeked around the corner. The coast was clear, so he waved to signal Marie.

She jumped up and ran to the corner of the avenue a half block away where Milo's pal, Angel, was waiting with his gypsy cab. She climbed in the back, directing it down Beverley Road.

Once it was idling in the front, Milo swiftly walked the length of the drive, and he dove into the seat as Marie flung open the rear passenger door. Milo gave Angel the address and sank back next to

Marie. He lowered his voice.

"Now I've just got to get Mal out of his place for a while. He almost never leaves unless he's posted someone there to keep watch. I've got an idea of who I can use – if I can find him and convince him it'll work. He hates Mal."

Supremely annoyed, Mal stepped gingerly down the steps of his door stoop, prodding homeless Stanley in front of him.

"Goddamn it, you got a lot of balls showing up here after the other night. You're a fuckin-A witness, my man. You're lucky if somebody don't *do you* before the day's over."

Stanley twisted round to protest. "Mal, that's what I'm trying to tell you. That's why I'm here. Those psycho Nam vets dragged me into that shit the other night! I don't give a shit what happened to Culkin. After I found out they been rippin' off the dealers, I thought to myself, 'Well, fuck them!'"

Mal was losing his patience. "So, tell me again, 'cause your dumb-ass little fairy tale is about as believable as one of those Times Square triple bills."

"I know where Milo is. You want him bad, right? I know the goombahs want him even worse."

"Yeah, but what about the really dangerous one, the older dude, what's'is name?

"Dave?"

"Dave, yeah, you know where he is?"

"Didn't you hear? They snuffed him night before last. Rizzo and the chink or whatever-the-fuck he is."

"If that's so, how come I haven't heard?"

"'Cause the whole goombah universe just blew apart. I know you heard that Nunzio got whacked, right?"

Mal looked away, nervously laughing. "Yeah, that's right. Shit. That kid, Anatoli, called and told me I could get in cozier with Carmine if I brought some flowers for Nunzio's daughter. Lot of good that did me."

"Call one of those scumbags if you don't believe me. I'm sure they'll be glad as hell to tell you they whacked Dave."

Mal didn't answer, thinking it over and surveying the block. One of his new street dealers was perched on the next corner. It was obvious that Mal didn't want to call anyone in the mob. He fixed his icy stare on Stanley.

"All right, you pathetic little dope fiend. You better know what you're talkin' about."

"Look, I'm not gonna swear Milo's gonna be there, okay? I'm just gonna show you where he usually stays. If he's not there, don't blame me. But at least, you'll know where you can find him."

"All right already. If you want a taste, tell me where he is."

"No, man. Gotta show you. That's the way it's gotta be."

Pissed-off, Mal bowed his head, aimed his piercing stare at the ground, then at his apartment window and finally settled it again on Stanley.

"All right, shithead. Let's find a taxi. Goddamn car's in the shop. I can't be out all afternoon."

Milo was in the downstairs hallway of Mal's building, watching from the partially frosted window next to the front door. He could plainly see Mal and Stanley scurrying down the block.

Milo knocked at Mal's door to make sure no one was there. After a minute of waiting, he glanced up the staircase, then down the hall to the open rear exit. Marie stood in the doorway in the narrow space between the building and the one behind it, and she waved an "all-clear." Satisfied, Milo knelt down before the doorknob, took out his pick and manipulated the lock. It clicked, and he opened the door. He was lucky Mal was so goddamn sure of himself and didn't have a more complicated security system.

18

At last, Nunzio's drawn-out funeral and burial came to an end.

The cemetery where he had just been planted looked as parched and dead as its occupants, almost as if it had been transported from Sicily's sun-scorched countryside.

Carmine was shocked at the dried-brown color of the grass. He led the procession alongside Sara, with Rosso, Scarpelli and numerous other mourners – both mob and family members – trailing behind them on the graveyard's dirt path.

Carmine had been sporting a scowl on his face since seeing Mal, and now he put on his sunglasses as they walked toward the late-afternoon sun.

"I still think it's weird that goddamn nigger showed up with all those flowers."

Sara lost her temper, but kept her voice down. "Goddamn it, Carmine, drop it!"

She glanced over her shoulder, worried someone would hear. "I told you, *I don't know why* he showed up. It's as big a mystery to me as it is to you."

They continued to walk in silence. The crunch of everyone's shoes on the gravel-strewn lane was deafening. A minute or so later, Sara removed her sunglasses and wiped her eyes with a handkerchief. She darted a sideways glance at Carmine.

"Just drop me at home. Thank God the wake's at Aunt Nina's.

Tell them I was nauseous and wanted to lie down. You'll be telling the truth for once."

He gave her a spiteful look.

Milo and Marie stood half-hidden behind a newstand near the intersection that was catty-corner to the Fiorile restaurant. Although it was hot as hell, Milo had the hood of a sweatshirt he rarely wore up over his head, and he tugged it forward to hide his face.

The red Lincoln Continental drifted by, veered to the curb, and an agitated Carmine disembarked. He bolted inside the café.

Milo kept one eye on the restaurant as he gave Marie her instructions.

"So far so good. I'm going to pretend to be a Fed and call the restaurant from that pay phone – " He pointed down the other street. "I won't be able to see what's happening, so I'll need for you to stay here and wave to me if you see Carmine leave. Stanley told me that Rizzo got killed the other night in a car wreck after they wasted Dave. But I'm not so sure I believe it. If you see Rizzo, or the kid, Anatoli –"

"The ones who were in the Lincoln, the other day, right? Who were giving me shit?"

"Yeah, that's them. Or if you see Yuen, the Vietnamese guy with an eyepatch – that happens, you come running for me, quick. Don't wait around."

She nodded.

Inside Fiorile, Carmine was talking to two muscular-looking men just to the right of the kitchen door. A waiter approached them.

"Phone, Carmine."

He was annoyed. "Who is it?"

"Didn't say."

"Get a number. Tell 'em I'll call 'em back."

"Said it was important. Urgent."

"Christ! All right. I'll take it in the back."

Carmine headed through the kitchen, navigated the obstacle course of bustling help and disappeared in the rear office.

He dropped down in the chair behind the desk, irritable and tired. A bright pool of light from a small oblong lamp on the green baize blotter was the only illumination. The rest of the room was in darkness. He yanked up the receiver and punched the one lit line.

"Yeah, who is it? What's so goddamn important?"

"Shut up, and listen, greaseball. I work with your buddy,

O'Reilly, you know the fat guy with the red hair who's always giving you a friendly wave?"

Carmine reined in his temper. "What do you want?"

"Me? I don't want anything."

"Don't give me that. You pricks from Justice always want something."

"Just thought you might like to know a few things. Things that we know. Like who really whacked your boss."

"You're wasting my time, fuckwad. I'm hanging up."

"Wait a minute, Carmine. I wouldn't do that. You won't get to hear about your girlfriend, Sara, and how she hightailed it over to Mal Power's pad as soon as you dropped her off from the funeral."

Carmine's face drained of blood. He was unable to speak.

"You still there, greaseball?"

He cleared his throat and coughed. "Go on."

"You should have seen 'em. I mean, it don't bother me, I believe in integration. But you guys are more old-fashioned. Let me tell ya – "

"Fuck you, bastard."

"Those big lips of his all over her. Right out on his door stoop before they even went inside. Whew. What a show!"

Carmine slammed down the receiver. He immediately picked it up again, dialed a number and waited.

Sara was lying on her back on her bed, a sleep blindfold over her eyes. She casually turned over as the phone started ringing, reached under her bedside table and unplugged the line.

Carmine let it ring 30 times – he counted – then smashed the receiver into its cradle.

"Fuck!"

Milo made it back to Marie in time to peer around the newsstand and watch Carmine fleeing the restaurant, jumping in his car, and screeching away from the curb, He hung a hazardous U-turn, which provoked honking from motorists, then swerved and careened around the corner right in front of the pair.

A taxi pulled up at the curb in front of Mal's building, and, after paying the driver, a very upset Mal erupted from it, followed by a defensive Stanley.

"Maybe you can go back to the cathedral when the cops aren't there – "

"You son-of-a-bitch! You didn't tell me that's where Nunzio got whacked, I'm not gonna cross a police line to track that cocksucker down –"

Mal stopped short as he registered Carmine's poorly parked Lincoln directly in front of his stoop. He nervously glanced at his apartment windows, then slowly started to climb the steps. Stanley dutifully tagged along, only to have Mal blow his stack and whirl around.

"Get out of here, motherfucker. I see you again on this block I'm gonna cut you up in little pieces!"

Stanley did an about-face and trundled down the street.

By the time he was in the shadowy foyer, Mal had his keys out, but he noticed someone had tampered with his lock. He lightly touched the door, and it swung inward, creaking on its hinges. About ten feet away, he could make out someone sitting on the edge of his massive bed, but he was in silhouette. In spite of his steely resolve, a spooked look spread across Mal's face.

"Hey, Mal." It was Carmine, scarily calm.

Mal remained frozen in the doorway. He tried to be cool. "What's up? What you doin' in my crib?"

"Come on in, don't be bashful. I need to talk to you."

Mal glanced at the scratched lock.

"That wasn't me. It was like that when I got here." Carmine's voice seemed over-friendly, and Mal didn't believe him for a second. Mal switched on the room light and tentatively stepped forward. He shrugged off his soft leather jacket and tossed it on the other corner of the mattress, onto the pillows, opposite Carmine. He warily circled the bed.

Carmine casually stood up, smiling at Mal, and moved to the door and shut it. A demonic grin transformed Carmine's face into a hellish rictus.

"Take a look under your pillow."

Mal was getting scared. "What?"

"Go ahead. It's not a booby trap. It won't bite."

Mal leaned over, trying to keep an eye on both Carmine and the pillow at the same time, and reached under it. He pulled back his hand, trailing Sara's sheer bra with the rose blossoms straps.

Carmine put his hands on his hips, pulling back the edges of his suitcoat to reveal a .357 Magnum tucked in his waistband.

"I was just wondering how that got there. Any ideas?"

Mal stared at the bra incredulously. "How the fuck I know? Some bitch's underwear. Must've been Darleen from the other night. I don't remember it, man. I was shitfaced."

"No, unh-unh. It's not Darleen's. Whoever the fuck that is. You know it's not Darleen's."

"What-the-fuck you sayin'?" He was trying not to lose his temper as he looked into Carmine's eyes. "How you know?"

Carmine very slowly withdrew the photo of Sara from his inside coat pocket, then stretched across the few feet to hand it to Mal.

"Because it belongs to *this girl.*"

Mal timidly accepted the photo from him, almost as if it might burst into flame at any second. It was the same photo Milo had taken from the Nunzio family album.

"You know who that is, don't you?"

Mal flinched. "That's…that's Mr. Nunzio's daughter, right?"

"Yeah, very good, Mal. Glad to see your memory is improving. The girl you gave flowers to this morning."

Mal became defensive. "Look, I got a call from one of your guys, one of Rizzo's guys, Anatoli. He told me I could get in good with – oh, shit!"

"No, it's okay, go on. Say what you were gonna say."

Shame piled up on top of Mal's anxiety. "That I could get back in your good graces if I did somethin' nice, you know, like bring the poor kid some flowers."

"I don't believe you, that Anatoli called."

"I swear to God, it's true, Carmine."

"You know why I don't believe you?"

"W-w-why?"

"Because I found that photo on top of your nightstand."

Mal started to shake like a leaf, all his macho bluster deflating.

"Somebody been fuckin' around in here, Carmine. Somebody fuckin' *put that shit here*. I swear on my mother."

Carmine just grinned, ignoring him. "You know what else I found?"

Mal managed to shake his head.

"Take a look under the bed."

Mal glanced down by reflex, then quickly up at Carmine.

"Go ahead, take a look."

At last, Mal summoned enough courage to stoop down. He refused to stop looking at Carmine and blindly reached beneath the bed.

His hand stopped, and his face went pale.

Carmine's patience was at an end. "Pull it out."

Mal dragged out the small painting that Milo had taken from the Nunzio house's basement. He stood back up, staring at it, not comprehending its significance.

"That came out of Sara's cellar. You're still not quite getting this, are you, Mal. Fuck, how did you ever move so much dope for us? You are one stupid nigger."

Mal bristled but was still petrified.

"Her father didn't know about it, no one knew…but Sara was…*is* my girlfriend. Now *you* know. And *I* know you've been fucking her. I've always thought she was a little tramp, but I never thought she'd stoop this low."

"No, man! It isn't true! Why don't you ask her?"

Carmine rested his hand on the butt of his gun. "Oh, I certainly will do that little thing. Right after I take care of your…little… red… wagon."

Mal clutched at his red-silk dressing gown that was draped over a nearby chair and heaved it on top of Carmine. He simultaneously dove for the refrigerator in the open-area kitchenette, yanked back the door and plucked out an Uzi. Before he could even aim, he wildly started firing. Throwing off the tangle of fabric, Carmine flattened himself on the floor beneath the spray of bullets, aimed his .357 and squeezed off a shot that pierced Mal's heart. Mal's gun arm abruptly slumped, and he went wide-eyed and slackjawed. Carmine smiled, stood and walked right up to Mal, continuing to squeeze off shots, riddling the corpse with lead and exploding a number of beer bottles on the lower refrigerator shelf. The bloody body was doused by an amber waterfall as it keeled over sideways to the linoleum floor.

Carmine shivered in the throes of bloodlust rapture, but approaching sirens nullified his euphoria. He raced to the nearest window and ripped back the curtains to see two police cruisers screaming from opposite ends of the block.

He was awestruck. "How the fuck – !"

He ran up onto and over the bed to flee the apartment, then tore open the building's front door, only to find that the two black-and-whites had already blocked in his Lincoln. Two more unmarked cop cars swerved to a screeching halt. Panicking, he slammed the door and whirled, running straight through the badly-lit hall to the rear entrance. The sounds of alarmed neighbors filtered down from upstairs.

When Carmine pushed on the release bar of the back door, he

became overwhelmed with terror. It wouldn't budge. Hyperventilating, he began to kick and hammer on the bar, then pounded on the wood finish, but it was to no avail; the door was immovable.

"Freeze, Carmine!"

Carmine spun around to face the voice. It was that plainclothes cop – what had Rizzo called him? That dumb homicide dick, Taliaferro. Carmine's skin was beaded with sweat, his mouth dry as he licked his suddenly parched lips, and his complexion was white with a super-charged fear.

Two more uniformed cops joined the detective. All of them now had their guns drawn.

"Drop the weapon, Carmine. I fucking mean it."

For almost a full minute, all that filled his ears was the sound of his own ragged breathing. Pitched at an agonizingly slowed-down, low frequency roar, he was suddenly able to discern the muffled noises of the onlookers outside in the street. Upstairs, some of the neighbors were getting brave and starting to descend to have a gander at the violence.

Taliaferro yelled, "You people upstairs, get the fuck back in your goddamn apartments and stay there." Taliaferro stepped forward and stretched out his arm to better aim his revolver. The uniformed cops followed his lead.

"C'mon, Carmine. Give it up. You can't get away."

"How'd you bums know I was here? It's fucking impossible – the way you got here so fast."

Taliaferro arrogantly smiled and drawled, "We got a tip."

Fury boiled over inside Carmine.

"Fuck you!"

He raised his gun and squeezed the trigger, but then realized too late that it was empty – he had used all his bullets on Mal. There was a deafening barrage of firepower as the cops opened up on him. He felt a series of faint pricks, then nothing as his consciousness was obliterated, and he did a jerky dance as he splattered against the rear door. When the cops stopped, his body remained erect for a few seconds, then finally tumbled face-first onto the hardwood floor.

The men in uniform raced down the hall, while Taliaferro calmly holstered his weapon and blithely drifted into Mal's apartment.

Behind Mal's building, a uniformed cop rushed down the narrow walkway between the structure and the next tenement over. He was surprised to find a huge piece of lumber jammed against the rear exit, and he heaved with some considerable effort to toss it aside so he could pry open the door. Once he was able to enter, he propped it open with the heavy slab of wood. He stopped to stare at Carmine's blood-soaked remains, then tapped the shoulder of one of the cops crouched over the corpse. The man craned his neck to look up.

"What's happening, Kowalski?"

"Jeez, talk about a goddamn fire hazard. Someone had that door wedged shut from outside."

"No shit?"

"Good thing for us, or he would've got clean away."

Milo, Marie and Stanley huddled between two cars across the street, behind a huge mob of gawkers that was rapidly gathering in the middle of the pavement. Worried, Milo glanced around the crowd, half expecting to see Yuen.

Stanley softly laughed and spouted a few clichés, much to his own amusement. "Well, all's well that ends well. Couldn't have happened to a couple of nicer guys."

Abruptly, he was off down the sidewalk.

Marie noticed Milo's anxious looks at the crowd.

She softly nudged him. "We should get out of here. He might show up any second."

Milo absentmindedly nodded, and the two set off to make the long trek to Dave's place in the Bronx.

19

Filled with apprehension, both Milo and Marie were skittish as they entered Dave's building.

Inside the freight elevator, Milo studied the control buttons before pushing the one for the fifth floor. The elevator noisily lurched upwards.

"Dave was going to reconnect the broken lock on this so it could be frozen in place, left upstairs and made inaccessible from the street level. But he didn't have time."

"What about the stairs? I didn't see any access to them up there."

"That's one good thing. For us, anyway. No stairway access. No fire escape anymore, either. The owner already dismantled and removed both for the renovation he's supposed to be doing later this year. He isn't even supposed to have anyone living here now. But Dave knew him from the war and talked him into making an 'exception.'"

The contraption was hellaciously loud, and Marie cupped one ear to hear better. Milo raised his voice.

"The thing is, if Yuen gets up there, we've got no way out."

Milo was stoic, but Marie gave him a fretful look. He wouldn't meet her eyes, instead staring up through the iron cage ceiling as each floor passed.

"Just remember what I said to do if we run into him. Don't walk forward or back away from him. Whichever side of me you're on, slowly walk sideways away from me in that direction -- "

"But –"

He turned to her. "Just do what I tell you. You walk away from me like that, it's going to do two things. One, it'll keep you from being hit by any bullets meant for me, and, two, it'll distract him. Which hopefully will give me a chance."

The lift ground to a clanking halt, and Milo and Marie wander-ed into the huge, empty expanse of room, searching the corners for any trace of Yuen. Milo stopped at the table and gazed out the window.

Marie came up behind him, encircled his waist with her arms and hugged his back, resting her face on his left shoulder. Both went rigid as there was the bang of a mechanical jolt, and the elevator started down. Someone was on the ground floor.

Milo disengaged himself from her embrace and turned to face her.

"Dave had some guns, didn't he?" she asked. "Where are they?"

"He's got them locked in the closet. I hope the key's on here."

He dredged up a key ring from his pants pocket, and he headed over to the door in the wall. Trying the first key, it didn't fit, and he nervously fingered the others until he found a more likely candidate. The key ring dropped on the floor. He flinched from the pain in his wounded left arm as he hurriedly crouched to grab them up. He lost his balance, fell against the wall and cried out as a blinding wave of fire ran up his left side.

He winced, wondering if his wound was getting infected. Remembering Saigon, he flipped a switch inside of him and brought the ache down to a bearable level. He tried another key, but it wouldn't work either. He fumbled with another, tried it, and it fit. He twisted it in the rusty lock, and the door sprung open. The elevator had stopped on what was undoubtedly the ground floor and then, after a few seconds, started back up.

Milo crouched, dredged up the canvas bag where Dave had previously stashed the guns, and rushed out to hurriedly throw it on the table. Marie held it open for him as he plunged in his hands to rummage through the contents. Both of them alternately jerked their heads to fearfully glance at the elevator shaft. The lift's cables coiled as the cage approached their floor.

He frantically tossed out the bandages and medical supplies. Marie was growing more scared, and her eyes tilted up to Milo. He became alarmed as it dawned on him that the guns were no longer in the bag.

The elevator noisily jolted to a stop, and they turned toward it as the door slowly yawned open like a mouth. No one emerged.

Milo looked over at the closet and spotted three shoe boxes on the floor. As she followed his stare, Marie noticed them, too, and she dashed toward the closet. Right before she reached it, Yuen's voice rang out.

"Get away from that bag."

They both swiveled in the direction of the voice.

He had just come around the side of the opening, his silenced automatic in his right hand. With his left hand, he reached in and pushed a button without pulling down the vertical safety door, sending the elevator lurching and groaning back to the ground floor. He calmly stepped into the center of the room, looking elegant in his eyepatch and designer suit, a model of sinister, sartorial splendor.

"I said to get away from that bag."

Milo and Marie did as they were told but also separated further apart from each other. Marie came to rest one step away from the closet

"You have no idea how much I relish this moment, Milo. How long I've waited to avenge myself and my poor sister."

"I wasn't the one who killed your sister. You know it was Jerry. And I wasn't the one who framed you. I loved Lucky. And she loved me.

Yuen suddenly became angry. "Don't call Loan that blasphemous American nickname." He paused, controlling his temper. "It doesn't really matter if what you say is true. If she hadn't known you, she might still be alive." He frowned. "I didn't travel all the way here to New York looking for you and Dave. It was for the benefit of my boss at home, hooking up with Carmine and his ridiculous bunch of incompetent hoodlums." He smiled ruefully. "I really have to avenge myself on you for that, too. You and Dave ruined the whole operation, delivered it stillborn before it even had a chance to live and breathe."

"Good."

Yuen laughed, and Marie nervously glanced at Milo.

"It was such a stroke of luck spotting you in that bookstore. An incredible coincidence. But I must admit that it's really unfortunate about your friend, Jack. I had no intention of killing him and didn't mean for it to happen. I liked him. He and I talked about 19th-century French literature, did you know that? Something I'm sure you could never appreciate."

Marie gave a sidelong glance into the closet, zeroing in on the shoe boxes.

"But your friend was the kind of man who always suffers for knowing someone like you. He was not the kind of American who ever had a say in his government's policies. It's Americans like you and Dave – "

Milo was getting angry listening to his self-justification.

" – who go abroad cloaking their real intentions of stealing, profiteering, killing and acquiring power in the guise of liberation."

"You hypocrite. You're no saint. You're just as bad as Dave ever was. Worse. Don't hide behind bullshit excuses. I didn't want to be there. I more or less got drafted. It was either that or go to jail. As far as governments, I don't care who they are, capitalist, communist, they're all a bunch of liars."

"Your last sentiments are very true."

Marie suddenly dove into the closet. Yuen squeezed off a shot that went *phht!*, and the bullet splintered the closet doorjamb. Marie's landing inside the tiny cubicle caused one of the shoe boxes to split open, spilling out money in unbound stacks of 10, 20, 50 and 100 dollar bills.

Yuen remained deceptively calm. "Milo, I want you to tell your friend to immediately come out of there."

Marie scrunched further into the closet and simultaneously opened another shoe box and peered into it. There was a gun, a .45, inside – in pieces.

"Shit!" She whispered to herself.

Milo stared into the closet and looked Marie in the eye. She mouthed something, but he couldn't decipher it.

Yuen took a tentative step forward. "Tell her that if she doesn't come out immediately, I'm going to kill you."

Milo said nothing.

Yuen raised his voice. "Girl, do you hear me in there?"

Marie opened the third shoe box and hit paydirt. She carefully drew out the 9mm, turning it over to see if there was a bullet clip inside.

She shouted. "I'm – I'm – coming… "

She plucked up a loose wad of cash, stuffed it into its box with her other hand and awkwardly stood erect. She tried to press herself back from the opening so Yuen couldn't see her, then she dodged out halfway, swinging the box so bills spewed into the air towards him. He fired, hitting the empty box, which flew out of her hand. Milo grabbed the bag from the table by its straps, heaved it, and Yuen pulled the trigger twice more, but this time the bullets hit the canvas satchel.

Milo tackled him at the waist, and the two plunged to the floor amidst the swirling cash. As they pummeled and kicked each other, Milo straightened out his injured left hand to hold Yuen's gun at bay, while he wrapped his other hand around the killer's throat. With a burst of adrenaline, Yuen rolled on top of Milo and slowly inched his gun barrel in line with Milo's head.

Marie, unused to the weight, held the 9mm with both hands, and she tried to aim for the best target on Yuen without endangering Milo. She prayed for the courage to pull the trigger. She had to make a choice. In mere seconds, Yuen would have a clear bead on Milo. Her finger spasmed on the trigger, but there was no shot. Shocked, she looked at the gun, aimed and tried again, but still there was nothing. Frustrated and desperate, she lashed out, bashing Yuen with all her strength on the back of his head. He tumbled off Milo, his gun flying from his grasp and clattering to the edge of the open elevator shaft. He winced, stunned to the verge of unconsciousness, and he seized the back of his scalp where he'd been struck.

Marie tossed aside her useless gun and dashed for Yuen's. He realized what she was doing, clutched at her, then ducked as Milo reached out to grab him back. Yuen caught Marie around one ankle, tripping her, and she sprawled on the dusty floor, clawing out for the weapon. Her outstretched fingers inadvertently propelled the gun forward, then over the edge and down the shaft. It clanked with an echo as it hit bottom.

Milo shakily stood up Yuen made it to his feet. Both eyed each other like wounded animals, Milo clutching his bleeding left arm, Yuen gingerly touching the back of his bloody head. Marie plastered herself against the wall as the two gravitated toward her and the elevator shaft. Yuen spotted Marie's seemingly useless, discarded gun. He lunged for the weapon, and Milo tackled him again. Both toppled precariously close to the shaft opening. Yuen, unaware of how close he was, kicked Milo away but propelled himself over the edge. Miraculously, he managed to grab the lip of the floor with both hands.

Milo regained his feet, and he edged closer. He crouched in front of Yuen, and Marie warily inched nearer, too.

Milo locked eyes with his adversary. Finally, he stretched out his good right hand to help pull him to safety. Yuen's sweating face was upturned, filled with hatred, his one good eye staring maliciously at Milo. Marie knelt beside Milo to help but, without warning, Yuen threw up his right hand, clutching Milo around the back of the neck and slamming his face down to the floor's edge. Milo gasped as blood spurted from his mouth, and Marie tried to pry loose Yuen's fingers. Yuen's other hand was gradually loosing its grip on the edge.

A glittery something tumbled from Milo's ripped shirt, hanging from around his neck. It was the pendant that had belonged to Lucky – the gift that Yuen had given her so many years ago. Yuen's eyes went wide with shock as he recognized the swinging medal. He gave an anguished cry, "Loan!" and grabbed at it. As he snagged the pendant, he lost his hold on the shaft edge, breaking the chain and ripping it away as he plunged to his death. The sound of Yuen's body hitting the top of the elevator five floors down reverberated with a dull thud.

Milo rolled onto his back with difficulty, and Marie collapsed on his chest. After lying there for several minutes, Milo managed to catch his breath, stand, lean over and push the wall button to summon the lift.

On the way down, they had to avoid the center of the elevator cage where Yuen's blood was still copiously dripping through the iron mesh top.

Outside on the street, the sun was setting, and Milo stopped and turned to face Marie. He pulled a large, folded wad of Dave's cash from the inside pocket of his denim jacket and handed it to her.

He smiled wearily. "You better be the one to hang onto this."

"Milo…" she started to protest.

He put a finger to her lips. "Ssh. It'll be safer with you." He gestured down the block. "I'm going to that payphone on the corner to see if I can get hold of Angel. He's supposed to be at a restaurant a few minutes north of here until nine."

Her heart welling up, Marie watched Milo as he headed for the phone booth, but she was distracted by the beautiful sunset against the New York skyline. When she looked back at him, he was just hanging up. He started toward her. Once he was about halfway, Marie noticed a man rapidly approaching behind him.

Suddenly, she recognized Anatoli.

She cried out just as Milo heard the footsteps and turned. Anatoli violently jostled him, then pushed on, stoic and nonchalant, steadily coming closer to Marie.

Milo looked bewildered as he slowed down and examined his stomach. For a few seconds, the looming figure of Anatoli blocked Marie's view. At first, she thought he might be coming for her, but the scary kid kept staring straight ahead, ignoring her as if he was in a trance, as if he had never seen her before.

Marie whirled as Anatoli passed, and she stared after him. Gazing back in Milo's direction, she saw he was still walking toward her, but his gait was erratic and reduced to a stagger. Increasingly frightened, Marie glanced again at the calmly retreating Anatoli. He jumped into a waiting sedan about halfway down the street. The car immediately tore away, burning rubber.

When she turned again to Milo, he was collapsed in a heap on the sidewalk. She broke into a frantic run, spanning the half block in a few seconds. She knelt down beside him and propped his head in her lap. He'd been stabbed several times, and his stomach was an oozing mass of bleeding viscera. He was gasping for breath and trying to keep his eyes open.

Milo blinked and, once more, his eyelids were like those twin, ten-ton iron shutters. Marie's face was blurring and changing. For a second, she looked like Lucky, then Anne and then Dorrie. Their faces blended. Then it was only Marie. He thought of Lucky, Jack, Dave and Culkin – all dead now, just like him. He seemed to feel his personality getting more diffuse, spreading thin. He felt there wasn't much more of him left. He was leaking out all over the sidewalk.

He was surprised to find himself relieved, not caring that much – except about Marie. She was going to take it hard. She needed someone, and he at last knew with crystal clarity that it wasn't going to be him.

His pale lips parted as he smiled.

"I told you it'd be better…if you took the money. You'd never have gotten the blood out..."

Tears rolled down her cheeks. "No, Milo. No, don't leave me!"

He looked at her one final time, then closed his eyes and died.

The sun had finally gone down all the way, and one of the only street lamps that was still unbroken came on, illuminating the blighted, deserted neighborhood.

Moaning with grief, Marie clasped Milo's head to her breasts and began to rock back and forth.

Thank yous...
need to go out to Donna Lethal, Eve Golden, Byron Coley, Lili Dwight, Thurston Moore, Eddie Muller, Kat Milne, Peter Maravelis, John Doe, Lydia Lunch, Grace Krilanovich, Mary Woronov, Jerry Stahl, Alan K. Rode, Alex Maslansky, Liz Garo, Billy Shire, Shepherd Stevenson, Benjamin Rew, Eleanor Whitledge, Erika Wear, Jane Reardon, Mike Minky, Richard Modiano, Claudia Colodro, Liz Faro, Tosh Berman, Patrick Paeper at Alias Books East, Mark Rainey and Julia Smut

Chris D. is the author of the novel *NO EVIL STAR* and the collection *DRAGON WHEEL SPLENDOR and Other Love Stories of Violence and Dread*. His anthology *A MINUTE TO PRAY, A SECOND TO DIE*, a 500 page collection of selected short stories, excerpts from unpublished novels and scores of dream journal entries, as well as all of his poetry and song lyrics, was published in December 2009.

His non-fiction *OUTLAW MASTERS OF JAPANESE FILM* was published by IB Tauris (distributed by Palgrave Macmillan in the USA) in 2005.

He saw release of his first feature film as director, *I PASS FOR HUMAN*, in 2004 (and its DVD release in 2006), and worked as a programmer at The American Cinematheque in Hollywood, California from 1999-2009.

Chris D. is also known as the singer/songwriter of the bands The Flesh Eaters, Divine Horsemen and Stone by Stone. He also was an A&R rep and in-house producer at Slash Records/Ruby Records from 1980-1984.

Other books include the novels *MOTHER'S WORRY, VOLCANO GIRLS, TIGHTROPE ON FIRE* and *SHALLOW WATER*, and the non-fiction *GUN AND SWORD: An Encyclopedia of Japanese Gangster Films 1955-1980.*

The life of recovering addict and Namvet Milo unravels when ex-CIA friend Dave goes off the deep end. Not only is Dave the heist man whacking NYC drug dealers, he's also hatching a scheme to plunder mob boss Nunzio's art treasures pilfered in WWII. Complicating matters, Yuen, an ex-Viet Cong with a grudge against Milo and Dave,arrives in New York.

"A healthy authorial sense of curiosityand generosity lends weight to NO EVIL STAR'S *intersecting lives, where Chris D. ably traces out the contours of human torment in a manner recalling American films of the 1970s."*
– Grace Krilanovich, author of THE ORANGE EATS CREEPS

AVAILABLE NOW FROM POISON FANG BOOKS

In Chris D.'s title novella, brilliant, alcoholic Anne, unable to succeed in downtown L.A.'s arts community, helps a Japanese-American girl escape forced prostitution, only to ignite a string of violent deaths. In "The Glider," a British policewoman falls in-love with a serial killer near the white cliffs of Dover; plus five more twisted love tales.

"...seems to shimmer with menace... with DRAGON WHEEL SPLENDOR, *the great Chris D should finally find the audience he deserves...a book that can kill the voices in your head - or make you love them."*
– Jerry Stahl, author of PLAINCLOTHES NAKED, PAINKILLERS and PERMANENT MIDNIGHT

The year is 1987, and outlaw Ray Diamond's mother is the queenpin of crime in Mystic, GA. After his Navy discharge, Ray knocks over a mob-connected El Paso liquor store, not counting on Eli, the owner's psycho son, dogging his trail. Back home in Mystic, Ray's girl, Connie Eustace, resorts to stripping at Mama Lorna's club to make ends meet. Witness to a murder by the local sheriff, she goes on a drug-and-drink bender, jumping from the frying pain into the fire.

"...a crazy dive into a universe populated largely by monsters...a classic update of the Gold Medal/Lion Library loser noir tradition. Great work..."
– Byron Coley, writer for WIRE magazine, author of C'EST LA GUERRE: EARLY WRITINGS 1978-1983

FROM POISON FANG BOOKS **AVAILABLE NOW**

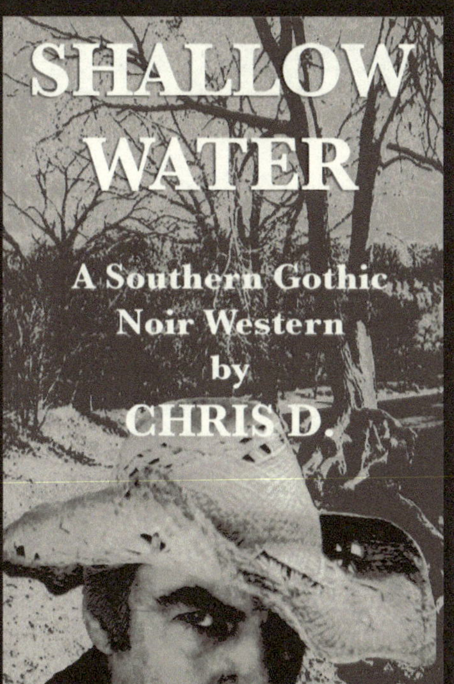

Post-Civil War, bitter rebel veteran and bounty hunter, Santo Brady, drifts through the Deep South. When he rescues halfbreed Indian prostitute, Lucy Damien, from one backwater town, he has the whole world fall in on his head. They embark on a freight-train-hopping odyssey to New Orleans, unaware that Lucy's rich white father and homicidal brother are tracking them. A tragic tall tale plunging head-first into a wild heart of darkness.

"One sinsister serpent of a story, an old Republic Pictures western serial scripted by James M. Cain and reimagined by Sam Peckinpah. I loved it."
– Eddie Muller, author of
THE DISTANCE and SHADOW BOXER

www.ingramcontent.com/pod-product-compliance
Lightning Source LLC
LaVergne TN
LVHW090955080826
845145LV00003B/1019

* 9 7 8 0 6 1 5 8 6 8 7 0 7 *